THOMAS BURNETT SWANN has a
style and vision all his own. His stories,
set in historical times, combine
myth and magic with recorded history
and give fresh insights into old
legends and mores.

Here, in WILL-O-THE-WISP, is
post-Elizabethan England, where
little pockets of non-humans cluster
together afraid, but in turn
frightening, fighting their 'difference'
by acts of terror . . .

Thomas Burnett Swann

Will-O-The-Wisp

CORGI BOOKS
A DIVISION OF TRANSWORLD PUBLISHERS LTD

WILL-O-THE-WISP

A CORGI BOOK 0 552 10358 6

First publication in Great Britain

PRINTING HISTORY
Corgi edition published 1976

Copyright © by Thomas Burnett Swann 1976

Corgi Books are published by
Transworld Publishers Ltd,
Century House, 61–63 Uxbridge Road,
Ealing, London W5 5SA
Made and printed in Great Britain by
Cox & Wyman Ltd., London, Reading and Fakenham

TO STELLA STEVENS, STAR.
Inimitable in beauty,
incomparable in genius,
love goddess to a godless age.

A novel suggested by the life of
Robert Herrick, poet, vicar and pagan.

Book One: Nicholas

CHAPTER I

'OUR new Vicar, Robert Herrick, to say nothing of staring shamelessly at the ankles of the comeliest maidens in his congregation, to say nothing of having included a poem by Catullus in his last sermon *before* the Twenty-Sixth Psalm, is perhaps, nay, probably, guilty of a crime for which the only suitable punishment is burning at the stake. *He is said on good authority to consort with the infamous Gubbings of Dartmoor.*'

Nicholas crumpled the heavy parchment of his father's letter and hurled it to the floor. It struck soundlessly on the rush carpet; he had somehow expected a thud. He collapsed into a chair ideally unsuited to the human frame (triangular seat, hard oaken back; his only chair, and rented at that) and stared through the gable window over the tennis court, the bathing pool, the orchard of Emmanuel College, that swelling fountain – some said nest – of Puritanism at Cambridge University.

Mercifully, he heard George climbing the wooden stairs of the building which was at once a library, a lecture hall, and a dormitory: George, who shared his rooms, who was not a Puritan, whose hair fell in golden ringlets around his shoulders. In spite of his dress, George was neither a fop nor a dandy; he was a robust young gentleman from Sussex who dressed with the elegance of his class when they attended college or went to London.

7

'George,' Nicholas cried. 'I want to do something – rather bad.'

George removed his cape and kicked a volume of Vergil under the bed. A slow smile ruddied his features ('ale-dyed features,' Nicholas' father insisted).

'You mean you want to let your hair grow long or wear a ring on your finger?' On his own fingers, rings glittered like bumblebees on stalks of rhubarb. He also wore earrings of hammered gold.

'Oh, much worse,' Nicholas cried. 'I – I've been having those dreams again. The maidens dancing around a May-pole, and – and—'

'I know, you've already told me six or seven times. One of them showing her bosom.'

'Both bosoms.' To no one else would he have confessed his carnal dreams. It was rare for the son of an apothecary to share rooms with the son of a country squire, but the crowded conditions at the college had compelled the ar-rangements and Nicholas had never ceased to bless the crowds. He liked George with the half-shocked, half-ador-ing affection of a pious, mannerly boy for a good-natured rogue.

'The word "bosom",' said George, whose knowledge of anatomy was as extensive as his knowledge of Latin was limited, 'may apply to a woman's entire breast, or to either globe. My application was to the entirety.'

'George, I'm serious.'

'Puritans always are. However, in this instance, so am I. There is nothing more serious, more sublime than a woman's bosom – or bosoms – as Catullus observed in his poem about Lesbia's sparrow and its favourite nesting place.'

Nicholas stifled a sob. As a rule, Puritans only wept when they fell from grace.

'Little friend, tell me what's the matter.'

Nicholas retrieved and smoothed the discarded parchment and read the damning words.

Even George did not jest about such matters. Not when men and women were being hanged and burned throughout the whole of England, as well as on the Continent, for conjuring the Devil or the Hag or their legions of demonic followers. When God had come to England with the Romans, the pagan gods had scuttled from field and fen, and the Devil, who gave them asylum in Hell, appeared to be permanently routed and tidily exiled. Now, however, as Anglicans, Papists, and Puritans wrangled over creeds and deeds and threatened civil war, he had clearly regrouped his forces and erupted from Hell.

'Consorts with Gubbings. . . . Not a light charge, is it?' He drooped sympathetically in his chair, which was square of bottom and cushioned with velvet (he *owned* his chair).

Indeed, it was a deadly charge. The Gubbings of Devonshire and its harshest region, Dartmoor, were not the little folk of Master Shakespeare's *Midsummer Night's Dream*. In the first place, they were witches and warlocks; in the second place, they were more than men and women who worshipped Satan and shared in his superhuman powers. They themselves were thought to be more than human. No one had seen them face to face, and they were variously described as hideous like Caliban (in order to horrify) or beautiful like Ariel (in order to ensnare), but everyone agreed that there was something bestial about them. Tails? Talons? Wings? Shadowy figures crossed the moors at night, but nobody knew if they crawled, fluttered, or flew. Only that they were evil – and powerful.

'Grim Devon,' George continued, echoing a popular phrase. 'Your county is well named. That time I visited you in Dean Church, I felt as if I were lost in Vergil's Hell. Soggy moors all over the place, roads too rough for carriages. And the light we saw the night of the wake – Your father called it a Will-o-the-Wisp. "Sent by the Gubbings". Remember how it tried to lure us?'

'Into a bog, no doubt. And did you know that my great-uncle was stolen from his bed when he was a wee child and a horrid creature with feathers on his back was left in his place?'

'A changeling! You never told me you had one in the family.'

'My father doesn't like me to speak of him. The changeling was drowned in a stream, but no one ever found my great-uncle.'

'But what has your vicar consorting with Gubbings to do with wanting to be bad?'

Nicholas lowered his head. 'I liked him. He's new, you know, and I only heard him preach once, at Christmas, but he invited me to the Vicarage with some of the other boys and girls, and I was the last to leave. We drank ale – oh, just a cup or two – even Father drinks on holidays – and he asked me to call him Robin. He's quite old – thirty-nine, I think – but he seemed, well, *young*. No beard, no wrinkles, hair like a sheaf of yellow wheat. And he writes poetry.'

'In other words, if a vicar you like—'

'Liked. I can't keep on liking a man who consorts with Gubbings, can I?' He really meant: I ought not to keep on liking such a man.

'Liked. If he can commit a big sin, then you think you may be allowed a little sin and God will be too busy to take any notice. That is, if you do it before you're ordained.'

'Exactly.'

'That's Puritan logic for you. Even when you sin, you have to have a reason for it. But do you know what I think, Nicholas? I think you've only told me one reason. You more than liked this Robin Herrick, you idolized him.' (An unfortunate choice of verbs. Pagan idols, golden calves, and all that. Accurate, though.) 'He probably reminded you of Catullus. Then he let you down. You're hurt, angry, disappointed. You want to forget that letter. You—'

'Will you help me to commit a little sin?'

George specialized in rhetoric. He hoped one day to become the Public Orator of Cambridge. When he began to talk, he did not like to be interrupted, but when his observations were uncannily correct, it was best to interrupt him. Yes, Nicholas had worshipped Robin Herrick. There was a goldenness about the man. You expected to find him out-of-doors and not in church. Blessing the sheaves of the harvest, not the wine of communion.

'How little? You realize that my experience is vast. I may be the third son of a country squire, but I've travelled to the Continent. I've spent a whole year in London. Was it a wench you had in mind?'

'Oh, no!' Nicholas cried, thrusting – or trying to thrust – the bosom of that disquieting dream back into its bodice. 'Not that bad. I simply thought that you might take me to the Devil Tavern. The name, don't you know. And all that tobacco smoke in the air. And blackamoors looking as if they had been scorched in the fires of Hell. And a mug or two – or three – of ale.'

'Why not a hogshead? Or perhaps some French brandy. In short, you want to get drunk.'

'Let's just say I want to roister a bit.'

'God's nails,' George laughed. 'Is that all you want? I roister six nights a week! Tonight you shall be my sole companion. Male, that is. I'll teach you the fine art of roistering.'

'But no wenches. I'm a slow learner.'

'Who else do you think will serve your ale? Call them barmaids if you like.'

'Barmaids are acceptable. I meant I only want to be served.'

'Good service,' George continued ruthlessly, 'includes more than setting a mug of ale on the table. Stand up, Nicholas.'

Nicholas stood to his full height of five feet and under George's scrutiny he began to feel like a calf being offered for sale at a Devon fair.

'You have the wrong colour hair for a Puritan. Even when you crop it, it's red as the Devil's backside.'

Nicholas blushed. 'My mother says its woodpecker-red. Most of the Puritans in Dean Church have hair that colour.'

'Same thing. As for your body, I've never seen you naked. You always bathe behind a screen.' So far as Nicholas knew, no one had seen him naked since he was a small child, and he had never seen his father so much as stripped to the waist. To a Puritan, an unclothed body was synonomous with temptation.

'But from what I can judge through that surplice, you'll do. A bit skinny. A bit short. Slight, one might say. But there's no accounting for female taste. Some of the girls prefer a little fellow.' George himself, though not yet twenty, was tall and inclined to the stout. 'And there's something in your favour. It's that confounded innocence. Those big green eyes that get round as a copper whenever I say "God's nails". Some girls like that. Just as some men like the blush of a virgin. It presents a challenge. It's fun, you know, to lead a sheep from the fold.'

'But not among wolves, I hope. When I said I wanted to roister, I did *not* include wenching.'

'You did not *say* wenching. But don't forget, I can read that Puritan mind of yours like Caesar's Latin.' It was almost the only Latin which George could read. 'Now the question is, when a wench sits in your lap and starts to run

12

a hand through what's left of your curls after your father sheared your head, will you know what to do?'

'I've read Catullus.'

'All of Catullus?'

'Yes.' His voice fell to a confessional whisper. His tutor had expressly forbidden him to read certain scarlet pieces about the poet and his relationship with the notorious Lesbia, whom Nicholas called 'that misguided lady', but who was better known in university circles as the Whore of Rome.

'Still, that's not the same thing as experience. The first time you notch an arrow you're not likely to hit the target. Unless,' he added, 'you can find a very easy target.'

'Sometimes you sound like a sailor!' Nicholas cried, half in anger, half in admiration. He had never met a sailor, but the cloisters of Cambridge were no longer cloistered and ever since the time of Henry VIII, British seamen had been renowned for their bawdry.

'I wish I had been a sailor forty-two years ago,' sighed George. 'And sailed against the Armada. I'd trade twenty pious Charleses for one lusty Elizabeth. Now what do we have? On one side, Bishop Laud with his rituals. On the other, you Puritans with your confounded consciences. Oh well, there's still London and Fleet Street and the Devil Tavern, even if Ben Jonson is flat on his back and Shakespeare in his grave. Come on now. It's almost roistering time.' He opened a chest and extracted a moss-green velvet cape, and a round hat with a large green feather, and a saffron shirt which could be laced to breeches which in turn were laced around the knees. A scent of camphor and storax pervaded the room. Nicholas recognized the clothes which George usually reserved for his visits to London. 'Now get out of that surplice. There's hot water on the way. You can have the tub first.'

'To think,' cried Nicholas, 'I'm going roistering with my best friend!'

He had quite forgotten the letter about his vicar. *'It is said on good authority that he consorts with the infamous Gubbings of Dartmoor.'*

'You Puritans,' chided George. 'You're sitting as if your chair were a pew. Even when you sin, you have to work at it. Didn't the musicians do anything for you?'

'No.' Such bands had been called a 'noise' in the days of Elizabeth, and the name, Nicolas thought, well described them.

At great cost but without even pausing to count his shillings, generous George had engaged one of the private chambers in the Devil Tavern of Cambridge, a small but rakish counterpart to Ben Jonson's famous haunt in London. There were eight such chambers, each of them opening into the large central hall, and each of them named for a Biblical demon. George and Nicholas occupied the Beelzebub. There was a pile carpet on the floor, strewn with rushes to catch the fragments of food which fell from the table; there was a little fireplace with andirons in the shape of grinning metal dogs; and the walls were hung with scarlet damask which flickered in the firelight like the flames of Hell.

Nicholas lifted his mug and took a large gulp, which burned its way down his throat and sat torridly in his stomach. French brandy indeed! No wonder England was often at war with France.

Soon, however, he began to feel as if he were warming himself by a fire on a cold night. Perhaps it was the quantity of ale. Perhaps it was his gratitude to George, who wanted so much to please him. Perhaps it was the fact that sinning was a cultivated taste, like tobacco from the Colonies. At first it stung; then it pleased; then it delighted.

14

The image of his father, stern in a black robe and broad-rimmed hat, came into his mind to shake an admonishing finger, but the genial George, forever refilling his mug, effaced the parental spectre.

'I really don't know—' he began, and he noted with pride that his speech was not in the least slurred – in fact, ale seemed to lend him eloquence. 'I really don't know why all this' – and he gestured to include the chamber and indeed the entire tavern, 'I really don't know why all this is forbidden to us Puritans. I find it quite Roman.' He pointed to the roast suckling pig, half reduced to bones, which lay in a silver platter on the trestle table. 'Might not Julius Caesar have dined on such a meal? Or Cicero? And aren't the ancients held up to us as models of behaviour?'

'You know what they say about Puritans,' said George. 'In the early days they were Satyrs. God was angry because they had such a good time. He took away their horns, he took away their tails "too much like the Devil"), he gave them feet instead of hooves. And finally he said, "This is your punishment. From now on you're going to have to behave like monks." But once in a while a Puritan reverts, and having a good time comes as naturally to him as swearing to a sailor. Do you know what you remind me of, Nicholas? Not so much a Satyr as one of those shepherds who danced with the Satyrs. There's not a wicked bone in your body, but there are several mischievous ones. You wouldn't organize an orgy, but you'd like to be invited. A hundred sermons can't quite smother the pagan in you – not while I'm here to play the pipes of Pan.'

'Would you say that I'm a real roisterer now?' asked Nicholas, swinging his mug – pottery rimmed with pewter and molded into the shape of a gargoyle – so freely that he sloshed a few drops onto George's lace cuff.

'Not quite,' said George good-naturedly, wiping his

cuff with a flowered silk handkerchief from Canterbury. He clapped his hands and, like Pan conjuring a Dryad out of a tree, summoned a barmaid. No, she was not a barmaid. She was not the shapely but harassed and worn young woman who had served their dinner of pig, brawn, charfish, venison in pastry, sparrow grass, and strawberry pudding. Nicholas recognized her as a street wench or, as George would have said, a 'dirty Dolly'.

'Dessert,' said George.

'I was quite happy with the pudding,' mumbled Nicholas, stupefied by this wicked apparition. The black dishevelment of curls, the golden loops in her ears, the excessive rouge on her cheeks, and the huge red mouth which looked as if it could swallow a young Puritan without even undressing him. Fortunately, for the moment she was occupied with cracking a hazel nut between her teeth.

'Chloe, this is my friend Nicholas. He's inexperienced but willing. Experience him, if you will.' George's departure was instantaneous. No goodbye. No parting advice. Neither barmaids nor blackamoors to shatter the silence, as tangible as tobacco smoke in the air. Behind a closed door which had suddenly come to resemble a portcullis, he shared the room with a half-eaten suckling pig and a painted giantess by the name of Chloe. If he rose to his feet, her bosom would be almost level with his eyes.

'Take a seat,' said Nicholas. There. He could still make conversation. He was still fortified with ale.

Chloe took a seat in Nicholas' lap. Good manners – or sheer lack of strength – prevented his ejecting her onto the floor, though he felt that she had taken an unwarrantable liberty. Women's laps were for sewing, men's for holding Bibles. Covertly he surveyed her bosom. To call it sizable was to do her an injustice. It was like calling the many-freighted Thames a rivulet. He tried to recall some suitable phrases from the Song of Songs. But Chloe did not resemble a Rose of Sharon. She was more like a scarlet poppy, full-blown, somewhat ravaged by wasps and bees, but still nectareous.

'Have some pig,' he continued.

'I've et.'

Nicholas felt at a loss for words; more serious, he felt at a loss for actions. A good host should entertain his guest. But clearly she was inclined neither to conversation nor to cuisine. How would they pass the time? Being a Puritan, he could not play the flute, only the harp, and somehow harping – even could he find such an instrument in the inn – did not seem to suit the occasion.

'Do you play the flute?' he asked.

For answer, she coiled her hand around his neck and lodged her fingers under his collar. He began to feel warm. Images pranced before his mind, the familiar maidens dancing around the Maypole, but all of them now had the face of Chloe, and they revealed much more than just their breasts. He had never seen a live naked woman, but once he had visited George in his father's manor house and found a garden of stone nymphs, however, but even the nymphs of his imagination had not prepared him for the nude amplitudes, both seen and surmised, of Chloe.

'God's balls,' she swore. 'With you shy 'uns, it's like picking the oyster out o' its shell.'

He sat quite frozen; no, baked was the word. He felt as if he had moved uncomfortably close to a blazing Yule log.

'Well, 'e *said* you'd need some coaxing. Best get the boots off first.' She knelt and, careful to avoid the spurs, removed the boots with forceful fingers. Then she proceeded to remove his doublet hose and rose-embroidered garters. He thought with a modicum of relief, It will take her several minutes on my collar and cuffs, and happily my shirt is laced to my breeches. (He was glad that he was not wearing a cod piece). All the time he felt as if he were getting closer and closer to the Yule log. Soon he would start to feel like a laurel branch which someone had thrown in the fire to scent the room.

But Chloe was impatient. 'What are you, a Johnny-Go-to-Plough? Be a gentleman and *help*.' She attacked the restraining lace as if she were a fishwife disentangling a succulent charfish from her husband's net. The lace was not meant to withstand the assault of thick, calloused fingers and Nicholas decided that departure, not hospitality, was the best course of action. He lurched to his feet, seized his coat, and, supporting his breeches with his free hand, stumbled out of the room and into the main hall.

'Score a pint of bastard,' one of the waiters was calling to the one-eyed man at the central bar, but waiter and one-eyed man and indeed the entire company of students and townspeople and visiting rustics, paused, so it seemed to Nicholas, to watch his flight, and he felt, even if he did not turn to see, an outraged Chloe watching him from the door of the Beelzebub. He skidded against a sideboard, dislodged a waterfall of pewter vessels, and staggered into the street with laughter cackling behind him.

George was idling under the sign across the street, a wooden antlered head emblazoned with the words 'Stag Inn' – the Cambridge boys called it 'Stagger Inn' – and evidently deciding if he should wait for his friend or resume his revels.

'George!' Nicholas shouted, stepping, no, leaping onto the cobblestones of the street. He meant to accost his friend, thank him for the roistering; reprove him for the wench, and announce his intention to return at once to the college and burn his volume of Catullus. He was so confused, however, that he fell to his knees. The air was dank with mist from the fens to the West of Cambridge and, far from clearing his brain, further befuddled him.

He saw but could not avoid the hackney coach as it clattered down the street, its black leather-covered body swaying like a huge mill spider. The driver attempted to rein his horses; quickly, much too quickly. The horse on the left reared into the air and beat Nicholas to the stones with his hooves. The carriage wheels did not run over him, and fortunately Nicholas was able to shield his head with his arms. But he felt as if his leg had been struck by a headsman's axe, and he heard the snap of a bone, a quick, brittle crunch like the snapping of a turkey wing in the hands of a hungry squire.

Before he lost consciousness, he thought: God is remarkably fast in punishing those who have strayed, even by one little meadow, from the fold.

God – or the Gubbings?

CHAPTER II

THE village appeared to be empty except for a sheep dog strayed from the fields, looking about him for sheep, and an old man who leaned on his crutches and nodded in the sun. The vine-covered stone cottages, some of them wall to wall, some of them standing separate like green hay ricks, lay quiet and muffled and forsaken by their masters, who had gone to the Harvest Home.

There were no customers in the shop of Michael Standish, Apothecary, the richest commoner in the town and the only father who could afford to send his son to Cambridge. Glass bottles, pottery jars, pewter bowls twinkled on the shelves. Opium, camphor, and storax. Rhubarb, cloves, and cinnamon. Tomorrow there would scarcely be a moment when Master Standish was not dispensing powder for a customer behind his counter, while his wife, as unobtrusive as a handloom in her skintight cap, her robe of black homespun, dusted shelves or emptied vials.

But today was the Harvest Home. Today he sat with his wife and son on the bench at the rear of the shop, beside the work table, beneath the shelves.

'I used a year's profit from the shop to send you to Cambridge. Did you know I had to pay double fees because you're a commoner?' Nicholas ought to know; his father reminded him whenever they met. 'And you have to go carousing with that rakish friend of yours, George Dunwich. Didn't I expressly warn you against him? However, Christ tells us that the Prodigal returned and was forgiven, and I am disposed to forgive you. The nature of your penance is self-evident.' He looked at Nicholas' crutches, his swollen leg – broken, badly set, still painful. 'Nevertheless—'

He paused for emphasis and assumed his Moses look. Small like his wife and son, he somehow gave the appearance of bulk and majesty. Though he lacked a beard, he might have been hewn from the ragged tors of Dartmoor. He had a way of standing with one hand slightly raised, as if he intended to hurl a thunderbolt or, in his benign moods, bestow a benediction. He had never struck his son, but neither had he embraced him. In spite of his red hair, he seemed to move in twilight and gather its shadows into the room.

'Nevertheless, though your leg prevents you from returning to Cambridge, though it appears that you are unsuited to holy orders and I must apprentice you to me as an apothecary, there is still God's work to be done. As you know, there is a devil among us right here in Dean Church.'

'Master Herrick?' Nicholas ventured when his father

stared at him like a headmaster awaiting the conjugation of a Latin verb.

'Who else? I wrote you about our suspicions. Only yesterday he remarked to the Miller's wife, "One of these days I'm going to visit the Gubbings. Since they won't bring their children to church to be baptized, I'll have to go to them." Now everyone knows that the Gubbings worship Satan. Furthermore, they are—' He paused, he appeared to grope for a word.

'Bestial,' said Nicholas' mother.

'Bestial. Beast men.'

'But how can I help?'

'He doesn't get on with many of his parishioners, Puritan or otherwise.' Herrick's church was Anglican, the only church in the parish, but several of its members were Puritans like Standish. The word 'Puritan' was a vague and general term which included Presbyterians, Congregationalists, and practically everyone else who was not an Anglican or a Papist. Often, through necessity or wile, they remained within the framework of the Anglican Church, the Church of England, whose bishops held the ear of the King. Michael Standish was a Presbyterian Puritan; that is to say, he abhorred elaborate ritual and devoutly believed that God's grace, not good works, exalted a man to heaven, though he insisted that a man must lead an austere and prayerful life in order to deserve such grace. 'But he likes you. I recall that he invited you to the Vicarage at Christmas and you came home reeking of ale.' The mug which Nicholas had drained with Herrick had been no taller than a toadstool. 'He will like you better since your accident. He has a foolish weakness for beggars and cripples. As if they were predestined to such an end! Win his confidence. Whenever possible, join him, follow him, spy upon him. In short, implicate him. We will do the rest.'

Nicholas' feelings about his vicar – he no longer allowed himself to think of him as Robin – were chaotic and contradictory. Surely his own accident was a punishment for liking the man; for using Herrick's apostasy as an excuse to carouse with George. Only last night he had dreamed his familiar dream about the maidens and the Maypole, but this time Herrick was with them, his lips twisted with sensual pleasure, his eyes glazed with drunkenness. And the maidens were no longer maidenly. They wore earrings of tarnished gold; they had painted their mouths; they resembled Chloe. Under their gowns he could imagine foxtails or feathers; *and he himself was with them along with Herrick.*

'He's at the Festival,' his father continued, as if to confirm the dream. 'You'll doubtless find him loading the hock cart. Or helping the maidens to load it. Go to him and *gain his trust.*'

Nicholas struggled to his feet; pain cut like a scythe through his broken leg. He lost a crutch and almost lost his footing. His mother rose from the bench to steady him. There was real concern in her pale, pinched features, her faded green eyes. Sometimes Nicholas wished that she would discard her white cap and free her dark red hair to catch the light. Once, unseen, he had watched her when she arose from bed in the morning and she had looked remarkably, almost unrecognizably young. But where other women heightened their beauty with combs and, in royal courts or Cambridge taverns, with paints, Esther Standish hurried to conceal her hair and grew more pale with the burdens of the day. A woman who exulted in the beauty of her hair, said Nicholas' father, might suffer Absalom's fate. Her pride would strangle her.

Standish restrained his wife with a hand which did not quite touch her sleeve. 'The boy does not need help.' Then, to Nicholas: 'Sometimes the flesh is mortified for the enlightenment of the soul. Go now to the playground of the Devil and accomplish God's work.'

'Yes, Father.'

THE town resembled a garden. Though the single lane was little more than a pig-trot, the stone houses, thatched with straw and lush with vines and flowers, looked as if they were grown instead of built, and the stone wall across the lane from the houses looked like an untrimmed hedge. Morning glory entwined with rose, blue flower with red or white, and sparrows bickered where in spring they had built their nests. When he was a little boy he had picked his mother a garland of roses from their own walls and she had smiled and hung it around her neck, but his father had come into the room and asked in his cool, even voice, 'Are you going to church – or a May Dance?' She had blushed and removed the garland, and it had seemed to Nicholas that, from this moment, he and his parents were divided from the flower-walled house, the town, the earth; that they ought to have built their dwelling with dark stones from one of the cairns in Dartmoor. Strange that Robert Herrick, whose vicarage above the town was a riot of roses, a haunt of larks and nightingales, should visit Dartmoor for doubtful, perhaps devilish purposes.

He suppressed the joy which opened in him like a morning glory and hobbled along the lane between the houses and the wall to join the Harvest Home and gather evidence which could send a man to the stake.

The celebrated grimness of Devon lay in its jagged coastlines and its mist-haunted moors, not in its towns, and certainly not in the opulent fields immediately surrounding the village of Dean Church, one of the three such villages in Robert Herrick's parish of Dean Prior. The soil was red and rich, the cattle were red and fat, the wheat grew as tall as Goliath, and during the daylight, at least, one could almost forget the brackish airs which sometimes blew from Dartmoor to the northwest.

Drawn by frisking fillies, the hock cart moved through the fields like a little treasure galleon, its riches the richest wheat of the harvest. The girls wore yellow bonnets, the boys wore sprigs of wheat in their blacker-than-crow's-wing hair. The manes of the horses were twined with daisies. Someone was playing a flute, and everyone was singing,

Crown'd with the ears of corn, now come,
And, to the pipe, sing Harvest home. . . .
Some bless the cart; some kiss the sheaves;
Some prank them up with oaken leaves. . . .

Herrick himself was leading the procession; in fact, he had written the harvest song. The cart lurched to a halt at the edge of a stubbled field, which lay like the back of the sheep from which had been shorn the Golden Fleece. Some of the elders were tending fires and roasting slabs of beef, mutton, and veal over the open flames, or scooping custards into dishes on rough wooden tables; or handing tankards of beer into eager, empty hands. An aged farmer, flushed and ale-eloquent, was drinking a toast to a pile of scythes and sickles and addressing them as 'my lovelies'.

At the sight of Robert Herrick, radiant with song and almost as youthful looking as the younglings he led, Nicholas felt the full hatefulness of being a spy; he felt as if he had eaten a Destroying Angel mushroom. There was something of summer about the man: wheat-yellow hair which enwreathed his head and tumbled, uncombed and unscented, about his shoulders. Wheat sprays stuck in his collar. Sunlight which kindled the goldenness of him to a brighter gold. His face was ruddy from the hours he spent in the Vicarage garden. His eyes were as clear and blue as a Devon stream in the spring, when it carried melting snows to the sea. He wore a tunic and buskins like those which the young farmers had worn in Devonshire since the Middle Ages, but neither stockings nor sleeves, and the silken, sun-glittered hairs on his powerful arms and legs gave to him at once a ruggedness and a delicacy. He looked like a man who could speak Latin and swear like a a coachman. He looked like a priest of Pan.

The song stopped; the young people scattered among the tables; and Herrick called his name.

'Nicholas, I didn't know you were back from Cambridge!'

Nicholas limped toward him.

The Vicar did not look surprised at the crutches. No doubt he had heard, with the rest of the town, about Nicholas' accident.

'Lean on me,' he said. 'I'll be your crutch. There's a bit of shade under that hawthorn tree.'

'Thank you, Master Herrick,' Nicholas said when he was seated as comfortably as possible under the tree. He was never truly comfortable, however, and he could hardly distinguish between the ache in his leg, sometimes sharp, sometimes dull and smouldering, and the ache in his conscience, an organ which to a Puritan was as tangible as a lung or a rib and in fact was thought to lodge directly below the heart. 'Now you must have some beer and beef. Everyone else is eating.'

'We'll have some together.'

They sat under the tree and divided a slab of ribs. Covertly Nicholas looked for signs of guilt – a furtive gesture, an air of secret depravity – but Herrick disarmed him with his blue, level gaze. 'The fill-horse is eating too. See, they've unharnessed him and he's nibbling grain out of the Miller's hand.'

'But the Miller's daughter – she isn't eating *or* feeding the horses. I think she's—'

'Tumbling in the hay with Scroop. You know what they say about Harvest Home. It begets more bastards than there are sprays of wheat in a hock cart.'

'Oughtn't you to do something?'

'I will one day,' said Herrick wistfully. 'Marry them, I suppose.'

A young girl strayed past them. Her sweat-damp gown, cut low in front to reveal the top of her breasts, clung to her body, as blatant an advertisement as the sign above the door to the Devil Inn. It was just such a girl who had prompted Nicholas' dreams about the Maypole. She nodded to Nicholas but reserved her smile for Herrick. Perhaps she hoped for an invitation to join them, or better, to replace Nicholas.

'Julia,' Herrick said. 'I see your friends are forming a Morris Dance. There's Jonathan dressed like Maid Marion.' An old, unaccountable, but inflexible English tradition demanded that a boy should play Marion. The Moors had originated the dance; the English had appropriated and anglicized it as surely as Shakespeare had anglicized Greek myths and Roman history. 'And see, George has stuck a feather in his cap. He must be Robin Hood. Why don't you join them? You could be the Queen of May.'

'But it's August, and it isn't even the time of year for a Morris Dance.'

'Never mind. Any time is right for a dance.'

'Will you be the Lord of Misrule?' She gave a coquettish and, so it seemed to Nicholas, downright simpering smile.

'Perhaps when I've finished talking with my friend.'

With a backward glare at Nicholas, she flounced across the field to join the dancers.

'I hear you're going to be apprenticed to your father.'

'For seven years. One day I expect I'll take over his shop.' He did not like to speak of the subject. He had never wanted to become a minister, but at least he had liked Cambridge. He certainly did not want to become his father's apprentice and spend the rest of his life mixing simples and measuring powders.

'It seems like drudgery, I know, dispensing all those powders and potions. But a good apothecary does much more. He learns to deliver babies as well as a mid-wife, and to set bones and, if he's really good, to treat the Plague. Speaking of broken bones, I'm sorry about your accident. You must miss Cambridge very much.'

'I do, Master Herrick. I have a friend there I miss.' Not for a moment had Nicholas blamed George for the accident with the carriage. 'And my tutor and my rooms and – everything.'

'I asked you to call me Robin. Have you forgotten?'

'No, I thought perhaps you had.'

'Forget my friend who knows Catullus better than I do? You may have had to come back to Devon against your will, but I think we shall have some good times together. You shall teach me more about Catullus, and I shall teach you – what would you like to learn?'

Nicholas forgot to speak as a Puritan. 'How to be a Morris dancer! How to catch a greased pig at a country fair! How to—' He looked down at his leg.

'About your leg,' said Robin. 'I think it's been badly set. I may be able to ease the pain. Will you come back with me—?' He did not have time to complete his invitation.

A cry resounded among the fields.

'A bear! A bear! Scobble has brought a bear!'

Bear-baiting was popular in London and even in Exeter, twenty miles to the north of Dean Church, but a bear in a small village was a rarity. Scobble, a loutish young fellow with as many warts as freckles, had dragged his animal across the field on a chain while prodding him with a shepherd's staff. Now he was chaining him to a hawthorn tree. The bear looked small, hungry, and unhappy; there was no chance of escape.

'George, Jonathan, Julia, Corinna, watch me bait him!'

George, Jonathan, Julia, Corinna, and most of their elders accepted the invitation. Meat began to scorch on the spits. Tankards of ale began to attract flies. One could always eat and drink or dance a Morris Dance. But a bear in little Dean Church – why, London had come to town!

Herrick followed the gathering with his eyes. Did he mean to join the crowd? Nicholas felt a moth of nausea, dusty-winged and fluttering, in his throat. Hunting was one thing. Every man and boy in Dean Church, if he could walk without crutches, hunted stags on the border of Dartmoor – when the stags hid in the hollows, their horns looked like bracken – or pheasants and patridges in the copses and fields. But to torture a chained bear! Nicholas knew the arguments. The sport was as old as the Norman Conquest. Bears were mindless brutes who deserved no sympathy. You had to beat them from time to time to show them their place. Still, Nicholas liked them. He did not want them tortured. He did not want his vicar to watch the torture. Or did he? It would simplify his task. He would feel less treacherous betraying a man who enjoyed such a sport.

It was then that he noticed the child. She had crept to the tree on noiseless slippers, a wee small girl with a black skirt and a white apron and hair as red as a brick fresh from a kiln. No such girl lived in the town or, so far as Nicholas knew, in the entire parish of four thousand acres.

The girl tugged on the hem of Robin's tunic. Her face

looked sad and knowing for one so small, but not resigned; no, not in the least resigned. She had come on a
mission and did not intend to fail. Her eyes were the green
of tender young grass dusted with pollen. Their color was
unmistakable because she never blinked; because she
stared fixedly, almost hypnotically from Robin to Nicholas and back to Robin.

'Please, Sir, will you help my bear? They are going to
hurt him.' The voice was small but precise; polite but
insistent and without that slight slurring which marked
the speech of the Devonians.

'Of course I'll help him,' said Robin, without wasting
time to learn how the child had come by such an animal.
He took her hand. 'Nicholas, will you wait for me?'

But Nicholas did not intend to wait. There was a bear
to be saved; there was a vicar who promised to become a
hero instead of a sadist. With the help of the hawthorn
trunk, he struggled to his feet, seized his crutch, and
hobbled after Robin and the child.

He arrived in time to see a gratifying conclusion to the
fight he had missed. Robin had taken Scobble across his
knee and was whaling him with the same shepherd's crook
which had lately prodded the unfortunate animal.

'And the next time I see you torturing a bear, I'll not
only throttle you, I'll chain you to a tree so you can see
how it feels!'

The crowd which had gathered to watch the baiting of
a bear was not disappointed; the baiting and beating of
Scobble, who was none too popular – he had a weakness
for poaching – satisfied their sanguinary expectations.
They had harvested the last wheat; they had eaten and
drunk and watched a bully whaled with his own crook.
They were easily angered, easily amused; roused to shout
or laugh or no doubt burn a man at the stake. Children,
he thought, whether boys in their belted tunics or old men

29

in trousers and kerseys. Whether girls who flaunt their breasts like a huswife her melons, or women who have no breasts to flaunt. I too am a child. But there is a man among us and if he is bad, there is much to be said for the Devil.

Robin rose leisurely to his feet and flung the boy on the turf, like a miller discarding a sack of meal. Scobble was heavier than Robin and at least as tall, but he looked decidedly diminished when he was stretched on the ground. Cautiously he regained his footing, ready to rumble if Robin should look his way, and blubbered across the field toward Dean Church.

Robin freed the bear, first from the tree, then from his collar, a crude dog-collar much too tight for his neck – it had left a large red welt. The crowd muttered warnings. Didn't the Vicar know that bears were dangerous? They bit, they clawed, they crushed between their paws. . . .

Freed of his chains, he lingered gratefully with Robin's hand on his head.

'There, little fellow. Go with your friend. You'll know where to find the grasses to heal your wound. The least we can do, though, is feed you. Corinna, fetch a slab of mutton, will you?' To Nicholas, at least, Corinna and Julia looked like identical twins, comely but bovine and stupid.

'If you please, Sir,' suggested the child, 'I thank you for saving my bear. But a tankard of ale would be agreeable too.'

'Your bear drinks ale?' smiled Robin.

Corinna tittered (or was it Julia? No, Corrinna. There was, after all, a difference in the size of their breasts). 'I'll fetch him some, Master Herrick. We'll make him sit on his haunches and beg.'

Robin ignored her. 'I have an ale-drinking pig in my vicarage,' he continued to the child. He had placed a steadying hand on Nicholas' shoulder, less to support him than to include him in the conversation.

'Actually, my bear prefers beer.'

'Is the ale for you then? Why, you ought to be drinking milk.'

'It's for my mother.'

Until that moment, no one, certainly not Nicholas, had noticed the woman who stood on the edge of the crowd. She was dressed severely in gray home-spun, her hair concealed by a hood and cap. She might have been a Puritan except for her expression. She was looking at Robin with naked adoration. A true Puritan would have hidden her feelings; indeed, would not have felt them except for God. Then she saw Nicholas. She stared at him intently, as if the sight of him surprised and pleased but somehow troubled her.

'Thank you, Master Herrick,' she said. 'My daughter, Aster, and I are deeply grateful.' The simple words conveyed more gratitude than a speech by the Public Orator of Cambridge. Her voice made Nicholas think of honeycombs from the woods and salt breezes from the Channel at the same time: sweet but not cloying. 'And your young friend too. He would have helped except for his crutches. Not that you needed help!'

'My friend is called Nicholas, but you already seem to know my name. And yet you're not from this parish.'

'Yes, I know your name.' Her gray homespun caught the light of her smile and seemed to twinkle like fine silk. Her eyebrows were crimson. One could imagine her hair as a tumult of roses, 'I am called Stella.'

'May I ask where you live? And don't tell me in a sonnet. You are much too real for the lady in Sidney's poems.' Sir Philip Sidney's sonnets, *Astrophel and Stella*, had been a favorite of Queen Elizabeth.

'In Dartmoor,' she smiled.

31

She might have said, 'In Hell.'

First there was a hush; then there was a murmur; then you would have thought that Scobble had reappeared with his father and sixteen bears.

'But nobody lives there except the Gubbings,' Julia cried.

'I live there.'

Corinna had returned with the meat, a tankard of ale, and a pout. Aster fed the meat to her bear, whose wounds had not impaired his appetite, and Stella received the tankard without embarrassment. Most of the women in Dean Church drank ale, but delicately, fastidiously, as if it were cowslip wine. She smiled, not to the pouting Corinna but to Robin and Nicholas, and she seemed to include the two of them in an arc of radiance.

'Master Herrick, will you drink with me?'

'Thank you, Mistress Stella.' He took the tankard and drank deeply of the potent beverage. Her lips had left a faint mark on the rim. He was careful to place his own lips in the exact spot. It was almost as if he had kissed her.

'And now you, Nicholas.'

No! he wanted to shout. I will drink after Robin but not after you. He could not categorize this disturbing woman. Women, he had supposed, were either Puritans like his mother or wenches like Corinna and Chloe. But Stella smiled at him until he drank.

'The three of us have shared the same cup,' she said. It was a simple statement, but she had the look of someone wreathed in daisy chains and leading a May Dance. Her eyes were greener than sparrow grass in the sun. 'Now we must leave you.'

Nicholas stared after them – mother and child, the bear between them – as they walked toward Dartmoor.

'Is she a Gubbing?' he whispered.

'I don't know,' said Robin.

'I think she is,' said Corinna, who had momentarily lost her looks. There is nothing more uglifying, Nicholas decided, than a mixture of malice and ignorance.

'Nicholas,' said Herrick, ignoring the accusation. 'Why don't you come to the Vicarage with me? Here, put your arm around my shoulder.' He was a powerful man, a ruddy, young-old giant who came from London but seemed a child of the country. He smelled of wheat and violets, of a new-mown field and a cottage which seemed to grow in its own garden. He had thrashed Scobble without losing his breath and could have carried Nicholas without slowing his pace.

'Robin,' Nicholas blurted at the risk of his immortal soul. 'Don't you know they can burn you for consorting with Gubbings?'

Robin laughed. 'Nicholas, the Puritans could burn me for half the things I do, and my own Anglicans for the other half. I won't burn easily, though. It will take a lot of logs.' Then he grew serious. 'You know, I haven't many friends here in Dean Church.'

'What about Corinna? Julia?'

'Oh, a few girls fancy me, I suppose, but it isn't my friendship they want, though that's all they get.' Nicholas believed him. 'The men and the older women generally stay away from me. They liked their last vicar. His sermons were plain as the homespun of their shirts and gowns. He talked about Heaven as if he had been there, and Hell as if that was where nearly everybody else was going except his own parishioners. But they tell me – your father among them – that I'm too poetical for a man of God. "God likes a plain-spoken man." How do they know? Aren't the Psalms poetry? And the Song of Songs?'

'I expect it's your naughty poems they dislike. The one about Julia's clothes and how you get her out of them. I

33

believe the last line runs, "Oh how that glittering taketh me!" '

'I didn't get her out of them, she got out of them herself. I spied her swimming one day. Anyway, it's all of my poems they dislike, not just the amorous ones. And of course they imagine all kinds of dark things about me. Should you even be seen with such a man? You might be endangering yourself.'

'No.'

'Why not?'

Nicholas could not tell him the truth about his mission. But he told him another truth.

'Because you saved the little girl's bear.'

'Suppose the girl was a Gubbing? Her mother too.'

'If they were, they weren't wicked Gubbings.'

'All of them are supposed to be. According to your fellow villagers.'

'But some of them aren't, are they?'

'Look,' Robin said, pointing to three solitary figures, a woman in a dark robe who ought to be wearing wheat sprays and daisy chains, a small bear, and a small girl as they crossed the gently rolling fields between hayricks and over streams, toward that sinister plateau of bogs and tors which was called Dartmoor. They had paused now to look back at Robin and Nicholas. The woman and the girl, almost simultaneously, lifted their hands in goodbye. The bear raised his muzzle. Robin returned the salutation.

'Nicholas, my friend. How would you like to go with me to visit the Gubbings?'

'I don't know,' he stammered. 'I expect I would be afraid. *Nobody* goes there.' Afraid, he meant, to discover damning evidence against his vicar.

'Except me. Think about it.' First we'll go to the Vicarage and look at your leg. Then we shall dine together. Then, tomorrow—'

34

'I don't think I can walk as far as Dartmoor.'

'We'll take my horse and you can ride pillion behind me.'

'A horse in the moors? He may stumble in all that bracken.'

'I can get off and lead him. What do you say?'

'Yes.' Slowly. 'Yes!' With growing excitement. 'I'll go with you!' He had made up his mind. Whatever he saw in Dartmoor, he would come back to his father and and tell such a lie as could hurl his soul from grace, to say nothing of getting his body burned at the stake. If it took a lot of logs to burn Robin, it would take very few to burn a thin little fellow like Nicholas. Still, he would have good company. The impious thought occurred to him that he would rather go to Hell with Robin than to Heaven with his father.

Robin gave him an affectionate hug. 'That's my Nicholas. I'll tell you this much. I never saw the girl or the bear or the woman before. But I think we shall see them again. There was something about her eyes—'

'A yearning would you say?'

'And a giving at the same time. She seemed to be asking for help, and offering who knows what in return.'

'Robin, has she bewitched you?'

'Yes, if you mean I can't get her out of my thoughts! But she isn't a witch. I'm sure of that.'

'But a Gubbing – they can be very beautiful, can't they?'

'So I've heard.'

'And dangerous. Some of them are said to lure men into bogs and drown them.'

'According to a very old tradition – it was the first thing your neighbors told me when I came here – the Dartmoor Gubbings are not so wasteful. They eat their catches.'

CHAPTER III

A little butterie, and therein
A little bin,
Which keeps my little loaf of bread
Unchipt, unflead. . . .

ROBIN'S poem about his vicarage chirruped in Nicholas' mind as they entered the cottage, large for Dean Church, small beside even the smallest manor house in the surrounding countryside. Built in the Middle Ages. It was timber-framed, with masonry between the timbers to guard the oak against moisture and decay. A parlor, a hall, a kitchen, and a butterie on the first floor; on the second, a gabled loft which Herrick called by the archaic term 'solar' because it caught the sun in the windows of both gables. There he slept in a trundle bed whose trundle bedded his innumerable nieces and nephews when they came individually to visit him; there he escaped to read Catullus and Horace and write the sermons which his parishioners considered too poetical. And there he led Nicholas, by the little gatehouse on its vaulted undercroft; through the broken wall which had once enclosed not only the Vicarage but a monastery now in ruins and reduced to a mound of wild roses; along a path edged with rosemary and thyme.

Low is my porch, as is my Fate,
  Both void of State,
And yet the threshold of my door
  Is worn by the poor. . . .

36

'You're such a tall man, Robin. Don't you bump your head on the lintel when you go into the house?'

'No, I duck. It helps to keep me humble.'

'You grow little flowers in your garden – forget-me-nots and sweetheart roses. Your bin holds hardly enough for the next meal, and you would rather eat two small loaves than one big one. You told me so yourself the first time I was here. Why is that? Your house fits me better than it does you.'

'I don't really think about such things, Nicholas. I suppose it's because I grew too tall too fast. When I was a child I used to lie on my stomach and look a grasshopper straight in the eye. Then I was suddenly so large that I was stepping on him instead. I don't want to step on him. I want to make friends with him, though it's hard now – I frighten him. I have to fall on my knees to get down to his level, and often as not he jumps away from me. Still, I can put him in my poems, along with a world where he can feel at ease.'

'And yet you're all the things a big man ought to be. The way you routed Scobble!'

'Hush, Nicholas. You'll make me proud. Don't you puritans say that pride goeth before a fall?'

'If you fall,' said Nicholas, forgetting his crutches, 'I'll pick you up. Do you know, this is the first night since I had my accident that I haven't wished I were back in Cambridge.'

'It's the first night since I came to Devon that I haven't wished I were back in London. My pig, Caligula, and I get tired of eating alone.' Caligula, a gift from one of his nieces, had come to live in the Vicarage after Robin had lost his sparrow Phil, a gift from one of his nephews, to a predatory cat (a Puritan cat).

The previous Vicar had lived in the Vicarage with a richly dowried wife and kept a maid in the gatehouse. But

Robin, of course, was wifeless, and he could hardly afford a maid on his salary of twenty-eight pounds a year. Thus he swept his own rooms, grew his own vegetables except for those brought to him by his parishioners, and, when his nieces and nephews were not visiting him, ate alone with Caligula. Tonight he served a simple supper of beets purslain, water-cress, and boiled eggs.

'I'm no cook,' Robin admitted. 'I just dump something in the kettle and light a fire.'

He was not being modest, he was being honest. But they had eaten heartily at the festival and Nicholas, for one, was so busy thinking about tomorrow's expedition to the moors that he hardly noticed the fare, except the water-cress, which seemed to him more fit for a duck than a man but which he ate out of deference to his host. They sat on wooden stools in the kitchen. A petit-point table cloth covered the table; pewter pipkins hung on the walls. A mouse, poised on one of the rafters, peered indifferently at the repast.

Robin had not forgotten his promise to look at Nicholas' leg. First he fed Caligula a mess of water-cress – there was a generous portion left from supper.

'Pigs are very clean if you give them a chance. Caligula is immaculate.' (He was not, however, odorless; Nicholas dreaded his inevitable expansion into hog). 'What is more, he's a watch pig. If the Hag ever tried to pay me a visit – in spite of my profession and several judiciously placed crusts of holy bread – he would let out such a squeal that she would instantly take flight.' His smile could not conceal the seriousness of the subject. Everyone in Dean Church, even a newcomer like Robin, kept a watch animal, generally a dog. No invaders, neither Hag, nor Satan, nor Gubbings, had ever been caught in the town, but in the time of Elizabeth a dauntless blacksmith had mounted his horse and followed a Will-o-the-Wisp into

Dartmoor and the next morning his horse had returned with a body strapped across the saddle, the nail marks of crucifixion in his hands and feet.

'Now we must get you up the ladder into my solar. There isn't even a couch in my hall. That's where I hear the complaints of my congregation. But there's the trundle bed upstairs. You'll never get up the ladder, though, on those crutches. Lock your hands around my neck and I'll carry you up on my back.'

'You don't think I'll drag you down?'

'If you do, I promise not to fall on you.'

Once in the solar, Robin deposited him onto the trundle which lay beneath and beside the larger bed, like a baby dolphin beside its mother. The mattress was thin but soft with eiderdown.

'Now take off your boots and britches and let me look at that leg.' Nicholas undressed with the double trepidation of a Puritan and a boy with skinny legs. But Robin was concerned with his injury, not his skinniness.

With careful hands he removed the bandage and surveyed the swollen flesh below the knee.

'I'm going to have to hurt you,' he said. 'Here. Drink this.' He opened a cupboard under a window-seat and handed Nicholas a large mug which he filled with wine from a hogshead. It was the potent Spanish wine called Sack.

'But I drank at the festival. And again at supper.'

'Yes. About a thimble full. Now drink.'

Nicholas emptied the mug with surprising ease and felt relaxed and genial. Robin explored the break; the pain was considerable but tolerable; it did not explode through his body; it did not shriek in his mind.

'The bone is set straight but not mending properly. And you still have an open wound. I think we can help it along, though.' He began to massage the limb with a plaster of dock leaves and iris roots. His big hands were surprisingly gentle.

'It's feeling better already,' said Nicholas.

'That's because you're drunk,' laughed Robin.

'Am I? Is it? Well, maybe a bit. Mainly, I think it's because you're so skilful.'

'I'm not even an apothecary like your father, much less a physician.'

'My father doesn't tend wounds. He doesn't like to touch people. The apothecary I had in Cambridge wasn't nearly as gentle as you are.'

'He wasn't your friend.'

Robin sat beside him on the bed. It was a chilly night; late summer nights in Devon were often chilly and there was no fire on the hearth. But Nicholas felt warm with ale and comradeship. It was time, he felt, to confess.'

'My father sent me to spy on you, Robin. To find out if you know the Gubbings.'

'I suspected he did, Nicholas, but I don't know them, and if I did, I don't think you would tell him.'

'But how did you know I wouldn't?'

'Because I like you too much. Love doesn't necessarily beget love, but friendship does beget friendship, at least between kindred spirits. You aren't really a Puritan, you see. You're a Roman like me. We love the same things.'

'But I don't like Caligula,' blurted Nicholas. 'He resents me and I'm afraid of him.'

'Never mind, you like bears and Morris dancers and—'

'Sack.'

'You see!'

Nicholas astonished himself by throwing his arms around the man. 'If you were *married* to a Gubbing, I still wouldn't tell anyone.'

'If I were married to a Gubbing, we might adopt you. If we could manage to get rid of your present parents.'

'I like my mother, you know. Maybe we could find a Gubbing husband for her – he might even let her show her hair – and serve my father to the wedding guests.'

'Most Puritans aren't very edible. All bone and no meat. Look at you, Nicholas. One good bite and that's it. Though I hope to fatten you.' (First he would have to find a cook.) 'Go to sleep now. Will the little bed be comfortable? Caligula has kept it warm for you.' Caligula was even now vacating the bed with an expression somewhere between vexation and calculation.

'You don't suppose he will tusk me in my sleep? I don't get on with domesticated animals. Either they urinate on me or they bite me.'

'Does your father like them?'

'No. He says they may be familiars. He never even let me have a dog.'

'Then you got your fear from him. All of your fears, I suspect. But if you'll let me, I'm going to put joys in their place. As for Caligula, he won't tusk you but he may try to shove you out of his bed. With your bad leg, I think you had better take the larger bed.'

'But the little one just fits me. Your feet will lap over the end.'

Robin would not listen to argument. He hoisted Nicholas into his own bed and, removing his tunic and bathing from a kettle of water which he had heated in the kitchen, he contorted himself into the trundle. He had to bend his knees and crook his head at an angle.

'You'll wake up feeling like a wilted water-cress. At least there's no room for Caligula.' His own bed was wide and comfortable. The glow of the Sack had not forsaken him. He wanted to talk.

'Robin?'

'Yes, Nicholas?'

'What you need is a wife.'

Robin's reply was prompt and terse:

Suspicion, discontent, and strife
Come in for dowry with a wife.

'*All* wives?'

'Most wives. Remember I'm a vicar. I visit people in their homes. I ought to know.'

'My mother didn't bring strife into her marriage.'

'No, poor thing, your father never lets her say a word.'

'She wouldn't say a harsh word even if he let her.'

'Probably not. But I couldn't be married to a black robe and a white cap. In your mother's case, I suspect that what's underneath is not unattractive, and I don't just mean her body, but I wouldn't want to take the chance. You understand, I have nothing against women. I like their hair. I like their ankles. I like everything except their wagging tongues.'

'Now my tongue is wagging.'

'That's different. You aren't talking about knitting or the price of yarn or the Miller's daughter whose baby is due three months after she was married.'

'Is your only objection to a woman's talkativeness? You could always tell her you had to think about your next sermon.'

Robin looked pensive. 'I guess I object to the *permanence* of marriage. Even if you loved roast suckling pig, you wouldn't want it every day, would you?'

'I'd soon get hungry for fish.'

'Exactly.'

'Have you often – dallied – with women?'

'Bedded down, do you mean? Not since I became a vicar. When I was at Cambridge, yes. Even when I was an army chaplain.'

'Wenches?'

'Ladies as well. You'd be surprised how popular the Cambridge boys are with the daughters of earls and dukes. With their mothers too. Remember, that was some years ago. Queen Elizabeth had only been dead a few years, and this confounded Puritanism hadn't grown into a Hydra. We had fun in those days. Still, things are not that different now, are they, Nicholas? I mean, there are still wenches. Or so I would judge from the Corinnas and Julias of my parish.'

'Are you going to remain chaste from now on?'

'I expect so,' said Robin sadly. 'No more duckling, no more fish. Except in my poems.'

'It doesn't seem fair to the ladies. I saw the way Julia and Corinna looked at you. Almost as if you were a hot meat pie. I don't think you're too old. Why, at thirty-nine you ought to be good for another four or five years. But as you say, you *are* a vicar.'

'But you aren't, Nicholas. What about you?'

'I'm not without experience.'

'You've had a wench or two yourself?'

'No,' sighed Nicholas. 'But one of them sat in my lap.'

'What did you do?'

'Tried to stand up.'

'I forgot. You're a Puritan.' It was not a reproach; it was a statement of fact.

'But Robin,' Nicholas protested. 'The Bible is very explicit about fornication. It was different for you until you became a vicar. You're built for that sort of thing. You must feel more temptation than most men, and tempt more too. No one's going to flash her ankle at me. I have to go looking for sin, and that makes me all the more guilty.'

'The Bible is inconsistent on the subject. Look at Abraham and his concubines. What is a concubine except another name for a harlot? And Solomon wasn't exactly monogamous.'

'I never liked Abraham or Solomon as much as I should.' It was a night for the truth. 'In fact I disliked them both very much.'

'I'm not surprised. Patriarchs, both of them. Like your father, in looks if not in deeds. How about David?'

'Oh, David is my favorite hero.'

'David had several wives, including Bathsheba, whom he stole from another man, and uncountable concubines.'

'But didn't you say you haven't fornicated since you became a vicar?'

'There's a time for everything, as the Preacher saith. I would disrupt my congregation if I started bedding the girls. The girls would be jealous of each other, the fathers would either beat them or me or burn us all at the stake.'

'At least you could look a little harder for a wife without strife.'

'I couldn't afford her on my twenty-eight pounds a year.'

'The happiest vicars I know are married. There's George Herbert over at Bemerton. His church is too poor for an organ, but he managed to marry and support a wife. She cooks for him, I hear.'

'Herbert is a saint. He brings out the best in a woman. I'd wind up with one who made me cook.'

'Still, I'm going to help you look.' Then he felt a tingling, not from pain in his broken leg. It was almost as if someone had entered the room on silent sandals.

'Nicholas,' said Robin quietly. 'Don't be frightened. But there's a light in the window.'

'The moon?'

'That's on the other end of the house. Besides, notice how this one bobs up and down.'

'Will-o-the-Wisp!'

44

'Yes. This time I'm going to follow it.'

'No, Robin, please don't go!'

'You'll be quite safe here. You can bolt the door after me and put a crust of holy bread under your pillow, and Caligula has wicked teeth, in case anything gets past the door.'

'But who's going to help you on the moors?'

'I'll carry a vial of holy water. Hang it around my neck. Then, too, I'm a vicar, even if not a very good one. I have some incantations – or should I say prayers – at my command.'

'Oh, Robin, you know that's not enough on the moors. In *their* country. Vicars are the rarest delicacy of all! You'll fall in a bog and drown or else be trapped and eaten.'

'I'll be as tough as a Puritan. There's meat on my bones, but it's all sinewy from walking and gardening.'

'Stop joking. I'm going too.'

'On crutches?'

'You think I'll slow you down?'

'I think you may get hurt. I can't let you take the chance.'

'I'll follow you then, and probably drown in a bog.'

Robin looked at him with searching affection. 'All right. You can come too.'

'We're going to find the woman and the little girl, aren't we?'

'Stella and Aster. Yes, I hope so.'

'Then she *has* bewitched you.'

'No. But I think she's sent for me.'

The horse was small, old, and tired from supporting a man and a boy. Also, he was frightened; there were no sounds, but chill gusts of wind set him to shivering, and his little hooves stepped tentatively among the bracken and heather. Even a penurious vicar could have afforded a younger horse, but this poor animal had been consigned by its owner, Scobble's father, to a meat pie and Robin had bought him to save his life. Bucephalus was more than grateful, he was worshipful, and there was probably no other horse in Dean Church who would carry not one but two masters into Dartmoor at night without even whinnying a protest.

Will-o-the-Wisp had led them for almost an hour, a far, small radiance now seen, now invisible, a sort of firefly erratically flickering but certainly leading them into the heart of Dartmoor.

'What is it, Robin?'

'A lantern, I expect. When it pauses, I can almost distinguish the outline of—'

'A very small being like—'

'The girl who lost her bear.'

Already they had begun to complete each other's sentences. 'I hope so. And I hope we're being directed and not lured.'

Bucephalus' hooves crumbled a clump of furze. Except for its yellow flowers – they had to guess the yellow in the dim moonlight – it resembled the skeleton of a plant, with spiny, brittle branches like fleshless hands. Soon they were riding among the tors, those rock grotesqueries which seemed to have taken root in a soil as harsh as themselves. The Gubbings were not the first to occupy these moors. Before the Roman conquest the Celts had built stone cairns and slab graves and an occasional fort, now in ruins. Who then were the Gubbings? Sophisticated Londoners suggested that they were escaped criminals or a little pocket of Celts untouched by the coming of Roman, Saxon, Viking, and Norman. But it was a London blacksmith who had ridden into the Moors with a skeptical smile and a promise to return with a Gubbing 'strapped behind me like a dead stag.'

'Robin.'

'Yes, Nicholas?'

'Do you believe in Hell?'

'I'm supposed to. I'm a vicar in the Church of England.'

'Do you?'

'No. Only in heaven, and not the kind with harps. In my heaven, men and women drink Sack and dance Morris Dances and never get married.'

'Hush, Robin! What if you're wrong? You'll open a pit at our feet!'

'I'll fall into it. You'll end up with the harp.'

'I believe in Hell,' said Nicholas staunchly, 'but if you're going, I am too. I suppose I can learn to play a flute.'

'I think we're there already.'

Will-o-the-Wisp had vanished among the tors. The glow from the moon lay like a bloody mantle on the stone outcroppings. The air was dank and moist, as if from a cave; brackish too from the bogs; wispily sweet at times with the scent of furze flowers.

'Robin and Nicholas.'

It was a woman's voice. She spoke their names with intimate familiarity.

'Is it Stella?'

'Who else? My daughter has led you here. Get down from your horse, Robin.'

'How do we know you for sure?'

A small figure, carrying a lantern, skittered behind the rocks. It was Will-o-the-Wisp.

But the capturing hands were not those of a child and the questioner was not Stella.

'Is it true what they say about you, Robert Herrick? That you found a village of virgins and left it a village of whores?'

CHAPTER IV

NICHOLAS was fully prepared for the earth to open her umber jaws and swallow them into the Hell of the Gubbings. Since his accident at Cambridge, his imagination had rioted like a garden of unholy flowers, Eden bereft of Adam. They will cast off their black disguises, he thought, and drag us into their warrens, their witcheries, their wantonings: a banquet hall supported by massive columns in the shape of May poles, garlanded with ivy and flowered with crimson poppies; Will-o-the-Wisps like torches illuminating the hall. In the shifting light, in the shadows of sin and pleasure, Maenads and Satyrs will drink from ramhorn cups; reel and sing and copulate. . . . And then the ultimate feast. . . .

But Will-o-the-Wisp was a little girl in a black robe and carrying a lantern, and there were neither tunnels nor banquet halls, there was a passage betweeen two tors, and a space like an amphitheatre, and the town of the Gubbings.

It seemed to Nicholas a town of absences. Absence of color except for the borrowed pallor of the rising sun: browns and grays and blacks. Absence of sound except for the slush of boots in the moist earth. The rough, sod-built houses resembled immense bird nests, but no vines softened the earthen austerity, no birds sang among morning glories. Strip away the vines, destroy the birds of Dean Church; blight it with winter to cold gray walls, and it was still a richness to this bleakness, a honeycomb to a wasp nest. This was a town which belonged indisputably to the night, and it seemed affronted by the sun; received its rays only to further bare its own unutterable barrenness. Even the black magic of the witch or the warlock was supposed to conjur demons of scarlet malevolence.

'Robin,' Nicholas whispered, 'the people look like the houses. I knew they might be evil, but I thought they would be – wondrous. I knew this might be Hell, but I expected orgies or demons. How can evil be so dull?'

Robin gripped his arm. 'There is something hidden here. It's as if the town were wearing a mask.'

Black-robed men, women in pointed hats and black gowns, opened their doors to look at them with no visible surprise and emerged from their houses to join their captors with a slow measured gait, almost as if they were joining a funeral procession. The tips of Nicholas' crutches sank into the soggy earth and he withdrew them with difficulty; he advanced with lurches and jerks. Robin stopped to help him.

'Get along, you womanizer!' Someone struck Robin's thigh with a shepherd's staff.

With a twist and a pull, Robin seized the staff, broke its oaken hardness across his knee, and flung the pieces into the papyrus-wrinkled face of the man who had struck him.

'We're not sheep,' he said. 'If you poke me again, you may well find me an ill-tempered bear.'

The man subsided into the crowd with a curious, crow-like caw; the others were content to lead, flank, and follow without in any way hurrying or even touching their captives.

The woman whom they had mistaken for the lady of the Harvest Home – the others called her Judith, and she appeared to be roughly equivalent to an Old Testament Judge like Deborah – paused in front of the one building which did not resemble its neighbors. It was built in the shape of an enormous crucifix, and of timbers instead of sod. The door and the windows captured in small the cruciform of the whole. It seemed a place in which to celebrate death.

In the shadow of her church, she looked at them with a regal and half contemptuous pity; she was no forgiving Mary, she was ready to judge and if necessary condemn two sinners who were so far beneath her, so tainted and soiled and unforgivable that the very touch of them would taint her, and yet she would still condescend to touch them if only her touch might save.

'I have brought you to our Tabernacle,' she said. 'As you may have guessed, it is also our place of judgment.'

'If we're to be judged, may I ask our crime?' Not even this place of shadows can dim Robin's splendor, thought Nicholas. He is an archangel. No, he is Apollo.

She smiled her remote, pitying smile. 'Robert Herrick, do you need to ask? Well, you shall have your answer. In the Tabernacle.'

The Gubbings, it began to seem, were no more than a sect of Puritans. The Puritans punished sinners by locking them into stocks or pillories, sometimes by cropping their ears, but human sacrifice, cannibalistic feasts, the sins attributed to the Gubbings – unthinkable! He ought to feel relief. Why did he feel a shivering down his limbs like the scurry of spiders? It was – what was the word? – the covertness of the place which chilled him. Behind their concealment of robes and silence, these seeming Puritans were either more – or less – than human.

The Tabernacle, though named for the famous shrine of the Old Testament, lacked its riches, its silver and gold; lacked even the simple graces of Robin's church. Robin's church was small and poor; its benches were hard and uncushioned. There was no organ. But there were always flowers on the altar – Robin brought them from his vicarage garden – sunflower and marigold and daisy. Daisies were his favorite 'because of their modesty'. And the light which flowed through the plain glass windows lit a large Bible in a gilt leather – a gift from Robin – on a table rimmed with a fretwork of wood which had cost – or given – some craftsman many hours of labor.

No flowers here; the Bible was black, ponderous; it rested beside another and equally forbidding volume on an unembellished table with stiff oak legs. The benches, black too, looked as if people could sit on them for a thousand years and never buckle their stern, sturdy legs. And in the nave of the church stood a squat cross, with a fully clothed, black-robed Christ whose face seemed to Nicholas that of his father or Moses. The only color in all the room was the blood which ran profusely from his hands and feet. Such an image, so large and centrally placed, might have smacked of popery had it not seemed the work of a dour, dutiful woodcutter instead of an inspired artist.

'And so,' she said, 'the Vicar of Dean Church has come at last to the church of the "infamous Gubbings". You won't find infamy here, however. Perhaps you will find the God you seem to have confused with Pan.' She was as arrogant and, to judge from her face, as beautiful as a male peacock. One felt that there must be plumage concealed beneath her robes.

'There's no joy in the place,' said Robin. 'You say I've turned God into Pan. You've turned Christ into a Puritan.'

She did not condescend to answer him; smiling, pitying, she stepped behind a pulpit like a black tombstone while the pews filled with men and women and began to resemble a rookery of silent crows.

But joy entered the place.

Stella and Aster were dressed like the others in death, but their faces were life. Among those hushed and sinister crows, they still seemed capable of song and joyful flight.

In spite of his fear, in spite of the place and the peril, Nicholas made a vow: If Stella will help Robin, I'll even encourage him to marry her.

Judith extended her hands in a gesture of benediction and then uplifted them in a summons to rise. The crackling of those stiff, innumerable robes was like the lumbering of crows from a field of grain. It was only Judith who sang, however. Nicholas had never heard this particular hymn, though Puritan hymns were sung in his own cottage. ('Because that Anglican vicar has no sense of pain. He forgets what happened between Christmas and Easter.') Exultance shone in her face; strong feelings were allowable when singing a hymn to God. Exultance and something closer to pride than any Puritan would have dared to admit. He wondered if she herself had written the words, their cruelty almost concealed in the smooth rhymes, the strength and resonance of her voice.

> *God, descend in wrath and fire,*
> *Burn the burnings of desire;*
> *Christ, who walked upon the sea,*
> *Salt the sores of lechery. . . .*

Judith began to speak. Her voice was stern and judicial but so far, at least, without condemnation.

'We have among us the vicar of Dean Church. Our friends in the village have heard him preach. They have watched him at the Harvest Home. They have visited him in his vicarage. What are the charges against him?'

'Insobriety.' The speaker was a hunchback. Nicholas recognized him from the village: Scope, the young Cobbler. Robin had bought a pair of boots from him because he supposed from his tight, bleached face that the youth was in pain.

'True, Master Herrick?'

'I haven't been drunk since I came to Dean Church.'

'Before then?'

'Several times. When I came back to England after the battle of Rhé, I was drunk for three days.' The English had sent an expedition against the French on the Isle of Rhé and suffered a murderous defeat. Robin, an army chaplain at the time, had helped to nurse the dying; he had even helped to amputate a man's leg.

'And in Dean Church you have frolicked with virgins at the Harvest Home and caroused in the Vicarage. True?'

'I have celebrated the abundance of the fields and the hospitality of the heart. I have drunk freely of brandy and Sack, even as Christ drank wine at the wedding of friends. But not once have I clouded my senses or faltered in my step.'

'You have lain with the girls of the parish.'

'Never!'

'Julia? Corinna?'

'Not one of them.'

'But you have lechered after them. You have gazed at their breasts with carnal longings. Only fear of exposure has held you back.'

'Yes, I have looked at them. Admiring their fresh young beauty—'

'Desiring?'

'Yes, desiring. I am not made of granite.'

'Flesh, fleshly. You stand self-condemned. And there are other crimes.'

'He plays a flute on Sunday.' It was the Cobbler's wife. Her face, once roseate and smiling, had been deformed by the Plague; she looked like a blighted rose-bud.

'He writes verses about fornication.' It was the Seamstress, a plump little owl of a woman who never ruffled her feathers. She might have been saying: 'He takes a walk in the morning.'

'And you, Nicholas. We are told that your father set you to spy on this man. Is it true that you sought his friendship at your father's behest?' She looked at him with a question in her eyes as well as her words. She seemed to be offering him a chance to save himself by disavowing his friend. She seemed to be saying: You do not need to become a martyr. We are not murderers, we are judges, and we wish to know the facts. He saw in that fearfully seeing eye of his brain the nature of a martyr's death. He saw the stake like the skeleton of a tree. He felt the thongs as they tore his wrists; the smoke acrid in his nostrils; the flames like climbing, scorching snakes.

'My father said that Robin – Master Herrick – was suspected of consorting with the Gubbings. I was to see if the charges were true.'

'In Dean Church, those who are not Gubbings believe us to be a remnant of the old fairy folk, linked now with the Devil. In other words, your father set for you a godly mission, even as Joshua sent his spies into the city of Jericho. Did you come with the Vicar to spy upon him? To see if the charges against him were indeed true?'

'No!' He thundered his answer like a Puritan condemning a sinner to Hell. 'I told him about my mission. He forgave me.'

'He forgave you. For betraying your father's trust? Thou shalt honor thy father and thy mother. . . . Why, Nicholas, why?'

'Hush, little friend,' whispered Robin. 'There's no need to share my punishment.'

'Because I love him.'

'You love a man you have known for a few days better than your father and your mother? Such capriciousness is hard to conceive. Unless you are one of those whom the angels of the Lord discovered in Sodom.'

He would have thrown his crutch at her if he had not

needed it to support his weight. He could only fling words, but he flung them like David hurling stones with his slingshot.

'If you burned me at the stake, I wouldn't betray him!' Then, quietly, 'I love him, but not like you say. As Jonathan loved David.'

'He's telling the truth,' said Robin. 'He thought me wrongly accused in the town. He came with me here to Dartmoor only to clear my name. You've accused me of drinking and lechery and writing bawdy verses. He's guilty of none of these things. He's the gentlest boy I've ever known.'

'Your sins have been enumerated. He stands condemned by flaunting his friendship for you.'

'Condemned by whom? What are you, Judith? You and your people? I have heard that the Gubbings are more than men. That they are—'

'Beast men? Master Herrick, I thought you would have guessed. The stories which terrify the good folk of Dean Chruch – it is we ourselves who spread them. That the Gubbings are "godless and bestial". That the Gubbings "eat human flesh".'

'And Will-o-the-Wisp?'

'A man with a lantern. Or a child, as tonight. Nothing more.'

'Why?'

'To frighten the curious, why else? We want no Englishmen lumbering through our tors to steal our tin or tempt our children into godless paths. Except for you, Robert Herrick. Indeed, we wanted you. We have wanted you since you first arrived in Dean Church. Your predecessor was a foolish but not an evil man. We tolerated him. In you, we hoped for one like ourselves. But we heard of your ale-flushed features; of how you swam in the streams by moonlight, naked and shameless, like

Adam before the fall. A snare for young women and so it would seem for boys. Yes, we wanted you, and we spread the charge that you were in league with us. How better to make you angry and curious? How better to lure you here?'

'You are nothing more than men?'

'God-fearing men.'

'I don't believe you,' he said. 'There is something about you. A secrecy. An *ancientness*.'

'We are simply God's chosen to punish those who do not fear and honor Him.'

'Apparently we worship a different God. Yours is a God of wrath and thunderbolts. He razes cities and drowns or burns his enemies. You've lost yourselves in the Book of Kings; you haven't even reached the prophets.'

'You will see, Master Herrick, that we are well acquainted with the Gospels. For example, with crucifixes.' She turned to the congregation. The faces were not, after all, identical. The Cobbler's wife did not resemble the Seamstress. The red welts on her face glowed like copper ingots in a fire. The Seamstress sat in smug, unruffled superiority. There, a farmer with vacant blue eyes who looked more puzzled than condemning. There, a child whose bright little moon of a face sat undiminished beneath its black bonnet (was it she who, carrying a lantern, had led them into the moors?).

'My friends, we must choose our punishment carefully for a man who has turned God's house into a pagan temple. Who seems, in fact, to have confused God with Pan. And for the Sodomite boy who, rejecting his own godly parents, has chosen to follow this self-avowed pagan.'

'Damn you,' Robin swore. 'Damn you, Judith, and all your sanctimonious Puritans. I've never cursed anybody except the Spaniards, but if you hurt my friend, I'll call on that God you seem to think is so ready with thun- derbolts, and see if he has one for you!'

Judith answered him with a wry smile. 'The accused threatens us in our own Tabernacle. Shall it be the stocks for him?'

'The stocks are for those who fall asleep in church or use God's name in vain. Sins, but petty. Forgivable.' It was the Cobbler's wife. Perhaps the Plague had made her a Puritan. 'A hundred lashes across that flesh which he so shamelessly bares. As many for his friend!'

'Too few! Too few!'

'What then? What penance to equal the guilt?'

'Perhaps,' said the Seamstress, crossing her hands in her lap as if she had just laid aside a needle and thread, 'the Ceremony of the Cross.'

There was such a hush as must have proceeded the eruption of Mt. Vesuvius or the fiery rain on Sodom and Gomorrah. Even Judith was momentarily dumb.

'So be it,' she said at last.

'So be it. The Ceremony of the Cross!'

'Is there any dissent?'

'Yes.'

The word tolled like a ship's bell, sweet but pen- etrating; indeed, irresistible. People looked at the speaker; stared and frowned at her. She smiled; she glowed. She might have been sculptured in bronze. There was bronze, too, in her voice when she rose to face the congregation.

'In our own Book of Redemption, a prisoner who is accused of a crime against God is allowed a trial.'

'We have already tried him, Stella.'

'In the Middle Ages, a condemned man was allowed a trial by combat. He was allowed to meet his accuser with sword or pike and prove his innocence or reveal his guilt.'

'I know the Book of Redemption by heart. There is no mention of trial by combat.'

'But there is mention of Trial by Rhyme. The poet Ossian defended himself against a man who accused him of conjuring Beelzebub.'

And Derleth thundered like the clashing of a thousand battle axes:
'Cursed are they who desecrate God's name.'
And Ossian replied, proud in the knowledge of his innocence:
'But to believers an undying fame. . .'
And so they continued, Derleth flinging his lines like spears, Ossian catching them in the steel-linked net of his words, until the poem was perfect and the accuser stood accused.

'This man is known for his facile gift of rhyme, his bawdy but artfully turned verses. Are you suggesting that if I lose to him, I myself shall stand accused?'

'Only that we should reconsider his punishment. And it hardly seems likely that you will be defeated. Haven't you graced our Tabernacle with the finest hymns since the Book of Redemption? You are his accuser and through you, God. Even if you were not yourself a poet, God would speak through you in order to condemn him. Unless we have judged him too harshly.'

Nicholas waited for Judith to silence this astonishingly outspoken woman, who dared to suggest that justice was not always to be found in a Tabernacle shaped like a crucifix. Perhaps, for reasons known only to herself, Judith did not choose to question.

'Very well then. He shall have his Trial by Rhyme. But I shall choose the subject. And if he fails to match my line and my rhyme in the alloted space of—'

'One drip of a water clock. Or so it says in the Book.'

'Then he has lost the trial.'
'And if he wins?'
'He shall keep his life.'
'And Nicholas?'

Judith shrugged. 'Nicholas too. He is of small worth, dead or alive.'
'And if he loses?'
'We shall raise their crosses side by side.'
'At any rate,' someone whispered, 'we'll get to eat their horse.'

Book Two: Stella

CHAPTER V

THERE were occasional mornings when she awoke in a
web of melancholy. Her ancestors had flown with the
eagles, but her contemporaries lived in cottages built of
sod; she had married a human sailor and lived with him
in Exeter, overlooking a harbor where, before she was
hatched, the *Ark Royal* had unfurled her sails and sped
against the Armada; but now she lived, a widow with a
small daughter and an aging bear, in a windmill which no
longer ground grain.

She did not encourage the mood. There were much
worse things than losing the power of flight: her people
might have grown to look like ostriches instead of Puritans. There were much worse things than losing a beloved
husband; never having had a husband to lose.

This particular morning she paused on the rush carpet
beside her bed in a guiltless pleasure of nakedness. I am
the only Puritan, she thought, and certainly the only Gubbing, who does not muffle herself for bed as tightly as a
bear in his winter coat. She kindled the coals on the
hearth; yes, this particular windmill boasted a fireplace
and chimney, her own additions to a room whose simplity
had once bordered on sparsity. A miller had built the mill
and lived here before her and Aster. Mistaken for a warlock in Dean Church because of his power over animals –
he had kept a bear in his cottage – he had fled to the land

of the Gubbings, who had tolerated him, though he was both a human and an Anglican, because he supplied them with flour. But tolerance was not the same as acceptance; he had ground grain and pined and finally, in spite of his bear, Artor, died of loneliness, leaving the machinery to rust and the bear to need a master; and she had returned from Exeter, adopted the bear, and metamorphosed the lower story into a room as bright and intimate as the nest of a lyre bird.

With the help of an exceptionally durable wagon and two stalwart horses, subsequently eaten by the Gubbings, she had smuggled a small treasure from her house in Exeter; hard joint stools of the kind which disgraced nearly every dwelling in Devon, Puritan or otherwise, but which she had graced with the fashionable new worsted material known as Turkey work. A tall-backed wainscot table-chair, whose back, when lowered into a table, provided space for pewter dishes and pottery mugs, for oat clap bread and rose tip wine. An oval cradle on wooden rockers, with oak-panelled sides, in which Aster's father had rocked her even before she had hatched from her egg, and beside which Artor, old, petulant, but grateful, stirred with ursine dreams. A chest on tall wooden legs, rather like a walking box, which bore a nef or jewelled ship freighted with spices, and a maple wassail bowl, its silver top entwined with lacings of gold, and a miniature wooden tree trunk hollowed to hold an altar to the woodpecker god Picus and Mother Goose, his favorite saint. Finally, at the back of the room, her clavicytherium, an Elizabethan spinet, with stool and keyboard and back like the spreading tail of a peacock. She had fashioned the room to dazzle the eye, to tease the ear; being a Gubbing, a bird woman, she saw and heard as sharply as a lark. (Like all of her race, however, she lacked a sense of smell, and the spices in the nef, though she knew them to be

61

aromatic – clover, cinnamon, storax – pleased her only with their colors and their textures).

She stepped onto the porch and looked above her at the four blades of lattice-work like enormous wings; if the wind blew, as now, the whole structure turned gently on a huge oaken post strutted to the ground. No longer did the millstones turn in the top story and grain flow through a tunnel slide down a shoot, and fall beneath the stones to emerge as flour. But the mill continued to turn even if not to grind, and she stretched the diminutive wings which sprang, like thwarted flames, from her shoulders, and remembered the old time, the time of flight. According to the Book of Redemption, a collection of ancient legends vampirized of their joy and infiltrated by the harsher commandments of Old Testament, her people were fallen angels, condemned forever, at least in the temporal world, to suffer and climb and atone. But she carried in her veins the blood of royalty; she knew that her people had indeed fallen from the sky, the victim of a plague called Feather Blight, but that they had never been those insipid angels of the folk who had conquered them. Today they were known as Gubbings, but once they had been the Skykings or woodpecker folk who had dwelled in Italy and England and built their homes in the branches of kingly oaks. Such facts were recorded in the Book of Rejoicing, a forbidden volume which she kept in her chest and guarded as if it were a newly hatched egg.

Most of the females of her race were drab, colorless beings; it was the males whose wings and plumes, though diminished (if not altogether vanished) were crimson beneath their black surplices. But Stella's ancestress had been a queen, and Stella's wings, however small, and her hair, a flurry around her shoulders, were as red as the richest roses which flames up the walls of Robert Herrick's vicarage.

She stretched her wings and remembered the not so old

time with Philip in Exeter. It seemed to her that the mill revolved backward in time until dawnglow became hearthfire, and Philip, her husband, her lover, lounged in front of the fire, flushed with brandy and flames. His ship sat at harbor, poised for the morning tide. But it was still evening.

He opened his arms to share his nakedness. There was a splendor upon him, a fire but not of the hearth. *And Zeus descended in a golden shower. . . .* 'Come, my Stella, my star, my witch. Loosen your robes. The firelight will clothe you.'

He had lost an eye to a Spaniard's pike; a sword had ribboned his chest. *But what a piece of work is man. . . .*

'I'm a fallen angel,' she laughed. 'Aren't you afraid I'll steal you away to Hell?'

'Afraid? Only of time. Why do you stand there, girl, chattering like some little huswife at her spinet?'

'Now you are safe,' he said.

'From the Spaniards?'

'Yes.'

'And the Gubbings?' She had told him about her people in Dartmoor and her flight to Exeter.

'Yes.' He cupped his chin in his hand and gazed at her with an admiration more intoxicating than ale. 'Your thighs are an inspiration.' Then the practical sailor replaced the lover. 'It must be the fusion of bones without air sacs around the pelvis.'

'Air sacs and pelvises! I wish I had never explained the anatomy of my race. You call yourself the last Elizabethan. Do you think Essex would have courted Elizabeth in such a fashion? If he had, he would have lost his head much sooner than he did.'

'I've already courted you,' he said. 'I've married you, haven't I?'

'And courtship ends with marriage?'

'Your thighs give harbor to my wandering pinnace. How is that for a metaphor? Blank verse too.'

'Worthy of Shakespeare! But you never wrote me a sonnet.'

'I'm a sailor, not a poet.'

'Never mind, I never wanted a sonnet.'

'An epic?'

'Firelight.'

But remembering made her sad. She opened her arms to catch the wind, a chilly lover at dawn, even to a woodpecker woman whose body temperature exceeeded that of a human by fourteen degrees. She preferred the sun, but soon the Gubbings would be about their work. Growing beets, she thought, with a wry smile; or mining tin; or cutting squares of sod for their earthen huts; or waiting a chance to spy on her and accuse her of shamelessness and invade her mill to condemn its riches; and, who could say, sentence her to the Ceremony of the Cross, a high-sounding name for crucifixion, in spite of her royal lineage. As it was, she did her work; she spun, she gardened yes, even beets – she attended the Tabernacle and the town meetings. She pretended to think that an England ruled by Puritans could redeem itself from the 'Bacchanalias of the bitch queen, Elizabeth.' She had suffered humiliations, even practiced hypocrisies for the sake of her nine-year old daughter, Aster.

But now it was almost as if she had learned to fly. She had met Robin Herrick. With the uncompromising, slightly rueful honesty which peppered her love of luxury, romance, wonder – rare dishes and exotic journeys – she assessed her body. I'm freckled, she thought, even to my toes. Philip said that I reminded him of a strawberry patch, and he always wished for a pail. But Robin may prefer a whiter skin. Some of these Devon wenches, though stupid as cows, are as white as milk. Furthermore, my breasts petite instead of voluptuous and, unlike that shameless girl they call Corinna, I have never escaped from my bodice. Even in the lost time, when a breast was for fondling as well as feeding, our wings could not support too generous globes. All in all, I am slender and small of bone – some of my bones are hollow!' – and if a man wants what they call in these parts 'a real heft of a woman', I am not for him. And my hair – she helped the wind to tousle it and appraised its silken texture – is it not perhaps too red for a man with golden hair?

In a phrase, she concluded, I am more than adequate but less than provocative. In a word, middling. I have had one husband, I loved him well and my body flourished beneath his care, but now there is a certain – indecisiveness – about me, summer threatened by imminent fall. Strawberries bursting on the vine, and no one to pick them. After all, I am thirty. I could choose a husband among my own people. But I would rather marry a Spaniard than a Gubbing or one of those louts from Dean Church – Scobble and his kind. (Several Gubbings had asked for her hand; if she had been proud, she would have admitted that much of the congregation – that is to say, all of the men – wanted her, and whenever she bared an ankle, a hundred souls threatened to fall from grace. If she had been proud, she would have admitted that to call herself 'more than adequate' was to call London 'more than a village.') I could crumple my wings beneath a gown and cloak, even as here in Dartmoor. I could walk to Exeter, as I did as a girl when I went in search of a husband. But now I have Aster. It is hard for a little girl to hide her wings when she is with her playmates, playing Hoodman's Blind or Trap Ball or Bear Leader. And wings mean witch in every English town, and witch means burning for the mother and drowning for the daughter.

But Robin was not in a town, he was in a village, and Dean Church, quite unknown to its lustier citizens, had been infiltrated by the Gubbings. She had met the Vicar in a way which reminded her of the old merry times when wonders were as numerous as sparrow nests in spring. Often she and Aster walked to the edge of Dartmoor and watched the farmers in the fields. The Gubbings dressed like Puritans – they were, after all, the first and the worst Puritans – and the farmer took them for strangers from the next parish.

Sometimes they lingered after dusk to watch the moon rise above the unharvested wheat. Before the coming of Christianity, the Gubbings had worshipped the moon as a god, not a goddess, and when he rose above the hills, he was said to be the daybird sun, sheathing his brilliance for the sake of his love, the nightbird Sirius. Swallows, moon-enkindled, wheeled in a Milky Way above their heads. Pisgies or souls of the dead, according to the Book of Rejoicing, which taught that the good might return as birds or animals to protect the ones they had loved. Lost souls, damned souls waiting to enter Hell, according to the Book of Redemption. But who could be lost in the light of such a moon?

'Mama,' Aster had whispered. Like 'Stella,' the name meant 'star', but Aster resembled a daisy, piquant rather than fiery. 'We aren't alone. There in that stream—' A multitude of streams spiderwebbed the whole parish. 'Someone is swimming. Is it a Merrow?'

The Merrow men, and this was decidedly a man – he wore no discernible clothes – were red of nose and green of teeth and quite insatiable for women, Merrow or mortal.

'Yes, I see. But he isn't a Merrow. You only find them in Ireland. And we mustn't spy on him.'

'Why not? We spy on the farmers and they aren't

half as glimpsy. He looks so alone. Why don't we join him?'

'I'm afraid we can't,' she sighed. 'If we took off our gowns, he would suspect our wings. Even beneath our petticoats.'

'Then let's stay and watch.'

'If you'll keep very quiet.'

'Quiet as a wren hiding from a cat!'

The stream meandered through a field of wheat, but there were copses of hawthorn along the bank, and a clump of sedges, used by the farmers as a source of bog hay, at the edge of the water. Stella and Aster tiptoed as lightly as quail behind the rushes. The moonlight touched the stream with ruddy fingers; there were cuckoos crying in the copses, a sweet sound to Stella, though Englishmen thought them cruel because they laid their eggs in the nests of other birds. The season was summer instead of spring, late for the cuckoos to sing their two-noted song, but she almost joined them when she saw the swimmer's face. But of course she did not dare to sing. Her singing was that of a bird, not a woman, or rather of a hundred birds – nightingale, lark, merle – opening their throats in a song so woundingly beautiful that a listener must stop his ears, like Odysseus with the Sirens, or break into uncontrollable sobs. No wonder her people were sometimes burned as witches! If he tracked such a song to its source, he might not accuse her but he would certainly question her. She did not fancy having to explain how someone dressed like a Puritan could sing like a Siren. Not to him. He was not a man to whom one could easily lie. The moon and the birds – he felt them too; he began to whistle the old folk song, 'Greensleeves'. If I could wear green for him, she thought, instead of funeral black! Would Philip take offense in whatever celestial tavern feasted his soul? Had he not said to her before he died, 'Don't wait too long

between hearthfires. You were never meant for the cold.'
She had waited nine years.

He stepped from the stream, a beardless river god – no
red nose for him, nor green teeth – and held out his arms
as if he were thanking the cuckoos and yet asking more
than they could give. But he was not Philip; he was
neither more nor less, he was himself; there was about him
the same manliness she had loved in Philip, but
a different, deeper gentleness. Not that Philip had ever
been ungentle to her. But this man, she felt, could
cup a sparrow in his hand and feed him sunflower
seeds.

It was going to be very hard for a while to open her arms
only to the wind, and she almost shouted 'No!' when he
stooped to recover his clothes. To imprison such beauty in
serge or homespun – a desecration! It would be like
caging a bird. But once he was dressed in tunic and
sandals, he might have been the woodpecker god, Picus,
except that his hair was gold instead of red. Perhaps he
was a phoenix god.

'Shall we call to him, Mama?'

Aster's voice was the thin, far piping of a cricket.

'Mama?'

'No.'

'Why not?'

'Because—'

'I know. Our wings. But I'm not afraid to take the
chance.'

They watched him in silence as he moved toward the
town, reluctantly, hating, it seemed, to leave the stream
and the birds. She felt as if the moon had set.

It was Aster who found the parchment, and the poem
scribbled in scarcely legible letters with a quill pen.

'See, he has left us a message, even though he never saw
us! Shall I read it to you, Mama? The villagers will see

our lantern and think we're Gubbings. Isn't it funny, we really are.'

To Robin Red-Breast

Laid out for dead, let thy last kindness be
With leaves and moss-work for to cover me:
And while the Wood-nymphs my cold corpse inter,
Sing thou my Dirge, sweet-warbling Chorister!
For Epitaph, in foliage, next wrote this,
Here, here the tomb of Robin Herrick is.

'But it's so sad. And yet he looked happy in the stream.'
'He was happy then.' She had seen his face. 'Too much so to carry such a sad poem home with him.' But what loneliness had brought him there in the first place, uncompanioned, to write his own epitaph? She knew him now to be the wifeless Vicar, he whom her fellow cubbings condemned as a womanizer and a tippler, both of which charges rather endeared him to her. (Philip had womanized until he had met her. 'How can you judge a lyre until you've plucked a lot of strings?' he had laughed. They had drunk from the same mug, and he had laughed again, 'Stella, I believe you could outdrink me if I gave you the chance.')
'We should have spoken to him,' said Aster.
'Perhaps you're right.'
'Is it too late to overtake him?'
'Now it is. Perhaps we'll meet him again.'
'Mama, I liked his difference. Those slim hips and that big chest. And the fine hairs on his belly. Almost like little feathers.' Her daughter had never seen a man without his clothes. 'Is that wrong?'
'No, Titmouse. How dull if everyone were like you and me.'
'Oh, I think it would be splendid to look like you. All

69

red and ivory. But we need the men too. It's as if we were ships without sails.'

'Or sails without ships. They support us, we guide them.'

'Yes, that's much better. But the other children say it's wrong for a man to look on a woman without clothes, and worse the other way around. They say the Devil lurks in nakedness.'

'Then they are ignorant and so are their parents. Sometimes I think that the Devil lurks in black homespun. In the old days, when England was almost as sunny as Italy, your own ancestors wore nothing except their plumage and their wings. The women were rather plain, on the whole. But the men – what a brilliance of feathers! Of course our wings have dwindled, and the plumage is gone from the females, and the men would rather be crucified than show the feathers on their backs. Still, there is nothing wrong with nakedness.'

They had met Robin again the afternoon of the Harvest Home. Aster had lost her bear, Scobble had found him, Robin had saved him – he and his young crippled friend, Nicholas. (How she had wanted to heal Nicholas' leg! She could, too; there were ancient skills for those who fell from the sky.)

'Mama,' Aster had asked on the way home from the festival. 'Would you like to have a new husband?'

'I don't know,' she had said without thinking, or rather thinking of Robin.

'I know I would like a new father. The first one didn't wait around long enough for me to know him. I meant to lose Artor, you know. Actually, I prodded him toward the Festival. I knew the Vicar would lead the procession. But how are we going to trap him? I saw you give him the eye, but he won't know where to find us.'

'I didn't give him the eye, I just thanked him. And we aren't going to trap him.'

'We'll have to. He doesn't want a wife.' Aster was a tiny child, like all Gubbing children; they had to be small to hatch from eggs. You might have taken her for six instead of nine. But she often spoke with the insights of a young woman.

'How do you know?'

'He has that wary look about him. He likes us but he doesn't quite trust us. Like a fine big stag sniffing the air for danger.'

'What makes you think I want to marry again?'

'I know you don't want a lover. You like permanent things. Clavicytheriums and pewter and wassail bowls. Besides, you could have had your pick of the Gubbings. I realize you're a bit on the elderly side, but even the young ones fancy you. Why, Timothy said to me only yesterday, when his father was digging radishes, "That mother of yours makes black look like scarlet. Sometimes I wish I were a Babylonian!" And he's only twelve.' Next to those famous Biblical wives, Sarah and Ruth, Aster's favorite heroine – and apparently also Timothy's – was the whore of Babylon. 'If you don't want a lover, you must want *something*. Or you wouldn't stand naked on the porch and look as if you'd forgotten you can't fly.'

'I have all I need. I have you. I have Artor. And our mill is prettier than any cottage in Devon – except the Vicarage.'

'And I have you, but I still want a father, and I'd trade the mill and live in a sod hut to get one!'

'Well, we aren't going to trap Robin Herrick.'

'Can't we let him trap us?'

But there was no time. Judith and her friends had lured him into their own trap. Now she could only sit on a bench in the Tabernacle and watch his trial and wait for a chance to speak.

She spoke like a queen.

CHAPTER VI

'MAMA, you were very brave. The way you stood up to that old witch, Judith.'

Old witch ... Judith was thirty, Stella's exact age.

'We haven't saved him yet, Titmouse. He must do the rest himself.'

Judith was leading the congregation to the town square. Robin and Nicholas, directly behind her, were flanked by two men who flourished pikes and tried to look like Michael and Gabriel. The path was narrow and straight. Its shape was deliberate – the Gubbings never wrought without a lesson in mind – and Stella would have liked to line it with primroses and recall the birds, the reeves, the gotwits, the curlews, which had departed from Dartmoor with the first missionaries. In the old time, everyone had built a nest on his roof for any ancestral spirit who cared to return as a bird. But the new time was hostile to birds, particularly, it seemed, to Robins.

'But will he have a fair chance?'

'I hope so. Judith is just according to her lights.'

'According to her shadows, you mean. I never liked her. She's jealous of you, Mama.'

'As girls we were very close. As you know, she wanted to join me in Exeter. Her parents stopped her, though. My own – your grandparents – had long since been caught with their wings in London and burned as a witch and a warlock, so I was free to go where I chose. Perhaps Judith envies me what I found in Exeter.'

'That's not the only reason.'

'Perhaps also because my ancestress is mentioned in the

Book of Redemption. If we still had kings and queens, I would be a queen and you would be a princess.'

'What I'm getting at, Mama, is that she envies you your beauty.'

'She needn't. She's really quite lovely, you know. There must be a touch of royalty in her veins. Bastardized, but still there. Her wings are larger than mine, and she hasn't any freckles. Or hadn't as a girl.'

'It's the way you wear your beauty. You look naked even in black. If we saw her naked, I expect she would look dressed for church.'

They had reached the square, the treeless, benchless, pathless place where petty sinners were locked into stocks ingeniously devised to accommodate hands, feet, and necks and to make their owners so exquisitely uncomfortable that, once they were liberated, a bench in the Tabernacle would feel like a velvet throne. The empty stocks, ranging in size to fit anyone from six to ninety, had a ravenous, ravening look, like wooden beasts with open mouths. It was not that there were no sinners in Dartmoor, but rather that the Gubbings were now so incensed by the sins of the King and his bishops ('tools of the Pope, that's what they are') that they had temporarily forgotten to watch each other for lesser sins.

If the stocks were an ugliness and affront, the water clock, so it seemed to Stella, was an abomination. Tall as a man, it was tarnished copper hammered into the shape of Christ on the cross. Every morning at dawn water was poured into an opening like a gash across his forehead. At precise one second intervals, a drop fell from either hand and plunked into the little pool, its bottom painted red, which submerged the foot of the cross in what seemed to be pallid blood. At dusk, when the cross was an inch deep in water, the pool was emptied for the night. The Romans had brought ingenious water clocks to Britain –

gods, beasts, vegetables. The Gubbings had refined them to this particular ingenuity of horror.

There was a space behind the stocks and the clock for raising crucifixes.

The congregation, which had assembled with a silence approaching stealth for judgment in the Tabernacle, was now as clamorous as a field of crows surprised by a farmer. Stella waited for Judith to quiet them with one of her Gorgon stares, but Judith was staring at Robin and she did not look Gorgonian. He stood superbly pagan beside the pool; unshackled among that gaunt menagerie of stocks, which seemed too petty to threaten him.

'Mama, do you see how she looks at him? If it weren't Judith, I'd say she was giving him the eye. It's as if she likes him but won't admit it. She's never had a husband, has she?'

'No.'

'A lover?' To Aster a lover was what the Whore of Babylon had enjoyed in abundance. A husband came to stay, a lover came and went. There was something to be said for lovers; you could change them as often as a town lady changed her gown. But only husbands made good fathers. Aster had made it clear that she expected her mother to catch a husband.

'Hush, Titmouse. She'll hear you and put you in the stocks. There's one for children, you know.'

'I ought to know. I've been in it twice for falling asleep in the Tabernacle. No, she won't hear me. She's too busy looking at Robin. And his mannerly red-haired friend, Nicholas. I rather fancy the friend for myself. I've always liked older men. If Robin wins, I wonder if Nicholas will wait until I'm – nubile – is that the word? And will he expect a dowry? Perhaps we could part with our clavicytherium. Mama, you aren't listening. And I'm talking about *husbands*.'

'I expect he'll wait. If Robin wins.'

If Robin wins – Stella did not believe in the Christian God. She devoutly continued to worship the woodpecker god Picus, who, however, was warrior more than bard and had never been worshipped for inspiring poets. Robin must depend on his own abilities as a poet, which were considerable, but also on how Judith judged them. If she rejected a single line, a single rhyme, he would lose the contest. She is usually fair, even if harsh, thought Stella. But I can remember her as a girl like me, ardent and hopeful. I found a husband, she found a congregation. If she has regrets – well, Puritans often reject what most attracts them.

Robin smiled to her. She saw his lips move in a silent 'Thank you, Stella.'

Her wings stirred at her shoulders. She felt an urge to fly, to sing, to— But this was not the time to flutter in her emotions. Her brain must be as sharp as her hearing. In such a trial, a rhyme might be questioned, a meter might seem to limp, and she must be ready to defend him against the congregation. She knew the extent of her power. Some of the men disliked her because she had rebuffed them. Most of the women envied her because she had married a sailor. But she had, after all, an ancestress who had been a queen in the Book of Redemption. The re-writers, the vampirizers had somehow missed that charming tale of how the original Stella, before her people had lost the power of flight, had spied a young Roman about to be sacrificed at Stonehenge, snatched him into the air and, after a suitable courtship, into matrimony. 'And her love was so great that her wings stood tall like flames. . . .' (It was doubtless the matrimony which had protected the tale from the censors. Indeed, it was a pleasing conclusion.) So – let them desire and resent her; let them envy her. But only she was queen, and a hundred black surplices, a church

75

like a crucifix, could not dissemble the fact that her people grievously lamented the loss of flight, of the old guiltless time when women had been heroines instead of judges.

'It is for me to choose the subject of our poem.' At least for the moment Judith had conquered her stare, recovered her eloquence. She was both accuser and judge. 'I choose the subject of – repentance.'

By the bill of the Woodpecker God, thought Stella (Philip had taught her to swear). How typical of the woman! She has never ceased to repent the fact that she did not go to Exeter with me. Robin, on the other hand, has nothing to repent except the lack of a wife (vicars ought to be married. They need a cook in the house. Otherwise, it's all beef and no vegetables. They need a mate in the bed. Otherwise, they settle for sluts like Julia and Corinna).

'Repentance and absolution. They seem unusually appropriate to our Vicar. The first he must learn; the second he may only hope for. I have entitled the poem "His Prayer for Absolution", and I propose a length of ten lines.'

A susurration of approval. An apt subject, an accurate title, a length which should not overtax the combatants or weary the listeners. Robin looked as if he had been asked to recite the Book of Leviticus. His devotional poems were far outnumbered by his secular poems, and he was known to write badly on the subject of sin. Never once had he mentioned Hell in his sermons, and only in his poems as an afterthought.

'Master Herrick, does the subject meet with your approval?'

'If it didn't, would it matter? Suppose I suggested Christ in the manger or grace for a child or. . . .'

'Don't try to sway us with your well-known honeyed sentiments. We too are lovers of children. "Suffer the

76

little children to come unto me." We too hallow the infancy of our Lord. But the dignity – might I say the finality – of the occasion demands a subject of greater seriousness. We have agreed then on my choice?'

'Agreed,' said Robin.

'No,' said Nicholas.

'What did you say?'

'*No.*'

'And have you a better suggestion, dear boy?'

'Harvest Home or Yule logs or Candlemasse Eve. Robin writes beautifully on such subjects.'

'Sublimity, not beauty, is our object here.'

Robin smiled. 'I will try my best to be sublime.'

Judith stared at his bare legs, splendid in the sun; his bare arms, muscled like those of a blacksmith; the archangel hair above the Fun face. Then, for the second time in the space of an hour, she lost her tongue. To Stella she looked like nothing so much as a love-sick cow; to her congregation she must have looked as if she were awaiting a sign from on high.

'It is for you to begin, Mistress, Judith,' said the Cobbler respectfully. 'We have all approved your choice.'

She bowed her head in humble assent, as if the Holy Ghost had suggested the subject. Abruptly, triumphantly, she raised her head and flung the first line like a gauntlet:

'For these my unbaptized rhymes. . . .'

Unbaptized rhymes . . . As if the Devil had inspired them instead of God. She was calling on Herrick to disavow his secular poems, his love pieces, his naughty epigrams, his celebrations of feasting and drinking – in short, the essence of his art. In five seconds he must match her meter and find a rhyme-word for "rhymes" and advance the poem toward completion in ten lines.

He frowned and lowered his head. One drop fell into the pool. Two.

(Picus, how can he think at such a time? But he has to think. To save two lives, he has to rhyme a lie.)

'Writ in my wild unhallowed times. . . .'

Judith nodded approval. The quick confession evidently pleased her. She chose her next words carefully. As the accuser, she was under no limit of five seconds.

'For every sentence, clause and word. . . .'

Inferior poetry. Like one of her hymns, smooth but wooden.

This time he groped and stammered before he found a rhyme

'That's not inlaid with Thee – with Thee—'

Stella's wings began to wilt at her shoulders. She counted seconds. Two . . . three . . . four . . .

'That's not inlaid with Thee, *my Lord* . . .'

'An imperfect rhyme.' It was the seamstress. ' "Word" and "Lord". You, Mistress Judith, would never permit such clumsiness in your hymns. It's as if I had dropped a stitch.'

Judith looked from the Seamstress to Robin, who met her stare with neither a smile nor a plea; almost, in fact, with a dare. He reminded Stella of Philip when he was dying of the Plague. He did not want to die, but he did not grovel for life. ('Stella, I wasn't made to play the harp. Do sailors and witches end in the same infernal tavern?')

'Let it pass. This once.' Then, rapidly—

'Forgive me God, and blot each line. . . .'

And Robin:

'Out of my Book, that is not thine. . . .'

And Judith:

'But if, 'mongst all, thou find'st one. . . .'

Mother Goose, what a line! It was worse than wooden, it lumbered. But 'one', at least, was easy to rhyme: 'son', 'done', 'fun' (no, not in a Puritan poem).

'Worthy thy Benediction. . . .' Robin carefully divided

the word into its five syllables to emphasize the last, rhyming 'un'. A boldness, even a license, but original and allowable. There was no dissent.

'That One of all the rest, shall be. . , .'

'The Glory of my work, and me.'

Ten lines, a finished if not quite a perfect poem. But the imperfections belonged chiefly to Judith.

And Judith was fair. If she could not recognize her own limitations as a poet, at least she must recognize the excellence of Robert Herrick. She graced the congregation with what Stella called her Madonna smile. (It meant that she was not sure if she would rather crucify a man or make love to him.)

'He has passed his Trial by Rhyme. He has saved his life and that of his friend. It is, however, unthinkable that we should allow him to return to Dean Church with his knowledge of our town. He must remain our prisoner.'

Stella loosened Aster's hand. 'Judith, is it not true that Master Herrick was lured here by a little girl whom he mistook – was meant to mistake – for my own Aster? And that you identified yourself as me in order to lure him from his horse?'

'It is true. Our good Cobbler attended the Harvest Home to note the behaviour of the vicar. He reported to us the curious incident involving your bear. We knew that Herrick had met you, drunk with you, learned your name and that of your daughter.'

'In other words, you deceived him, and used my name and Aster's in your deceit.'

'Again yes. My namesake, Judith, deceived Holofernes in order to behead him in the name of the Lord. God may approve a strategem to deal with his enemies.'

'Robert Herrick has just proved that he is not God's enemy.'

'I have told you why he must stay with us here in Dartmoor. What are you suggesting, Stella?'

It was unsettling to hear her name spoken by a woman who had once been her friend – with familiarity but not with friendliness. Could a generous girl grow altogether into a hard woman in eleven years? Or did that same young girl hide somewhere in the bell tower of the woman's mind, peeping through a window, peering down a ladder?

'That he and Nicholas be placed in the custody of those whose names were used to lead him here. That they become my prisoners. The mill has ground no flour for many years, and not one of you can set its machinery aright.' (Actually, since occupying the mill, she had not allowed them to try; in order to reach the machinery, they must pass through her houseplace and spy her forbidden luxuries.) 'I will put them to work as millers. Then you can forget your hand-mills and devote more time to growing beets and radishes.'

'They have only to flee across the moors to Dean Church.'

'Aster and I will stand surety for them.'

'I recall, Stella, that you yourself once forsook us and sought a husband in that sailors' brothel known as Exeter.'

She resisted the urge to say: And you would have joined me if your father had not discovered your plans and locked you in the stocks. She said: 'And I returned as a widow to prove my loyalty by nine years in which I have out-worked every woman in Dartmoor. Weaving. Gardening, Sewing. Who sewed the robe you're wearing?'

'You did.'

'Is it well sewn?'

'It will pass. As long as our dear seamstress must sew for the people of Dean Church.'

'Did I not grow the largest pumpkins in Dartmoor last year?

'Size is not always a measure of excellence. But yes, you did.'

'When I left Dartmoor as a girl, I broke no rule. Nothing in the Scriptures or the Book of Redemption forbids us to visit the world beyond these tors. Our 'dear Seamstress' rarely visits us here in Dartmoor. The Miller and his wife – how often do they grace our Tabernacle? You yourself have been to London.'

'On God's work.'

'And I lived a godly life in Exeter. I was wed, I bore a child. It is true that the man of my choice was not then a Puritan, but it was in my heart to make him one and bring him back with me to Dartmoor. I showed him my wings before we were wed – at the risk of seeming a witch – and told him my purpose. One more voyage he died of the Plague.' (By the crest of Picus, by the eggs of Mother Goose, may Philip's ghost not hear me. No, let him hear! It will give him a laugh in his celestial tavern.)

'I don't question your integrity, Stella. I question the propriety of your sharing a mill with a man who is not your husband and a boy who is not your son.'

'Very well. They shall sleep beneath the mill. I shall be the miller, and he and Nicholas shall be my apprentices. Where else do apprentices sleep? Do you suggest that I am prompted by carnal longings? An injustice has been done to a man and a boy *in my name*. As you say, they must remain our prisoners. But allow me to atone for the anguish we have caused them. I will give them shelter and gainful employment. I will do my best to convert them to our ways. And with their help I will bake you the best bread this side of London!'

The Gubbings enjoyed few niceties at the table; they were poor farmers and impossible bakers; and their usual fare was heavy clap bread which would offend an undiscriminating pig. Stella's offer was greeted by a unanimity of approval. The Cobbler clapped his hands. More time for him in which to mend soles! The Seamstress clucked with pleased expectancy. More time for her in which to sew!

'Master Herrick, what do you think of this scheme proposed by your benefactress?'

'When I was a boy, I visited my uncle in a Charnwood Forest. There was a mill on his land. I worked it for a whole summer. Yes, Nicholas and I will gladly go with Mistress Stella. And we thank you for your justice.'

'Go with her then with our blessing. But go no further.'

Stella assumed a dutiful mask. 'Come, Master Herrick. Come, Nicholas. There is rust to scrape. Flour to be ground. Bread to be baked.'

'See that you bake well, Stella.'

When she turned her back, Stella felt Judith's stare like a scorpion on her wings and remembered the girl who had wanted to go to Exeter. ('Stella, will we really find husbands? I want a sailor with golden hair and arms as thick as the masts on a brigantine!')

Now Judith had two grievances against her.

Her ancestors had flown with the eagles, but her contemporaries lived in cottages built of sod. She had married a human sailor, PHILIP, been widowed, and now lived once more in Dartmoor among her people, the Gubbings, with her small daughter and an aging bear in a windmill which no longer ground grain.

Stella carried in her veins the blood of royalty; from her shoulders diminutive wings sprang like thwarted flames. According to the Book of Redemption, a collection of ancient legends vampirized of their joy and infiltrated by the harsher commandments of the Old Testament, her people were fallen angels, condemned forever, at least in the temporal world, to suffer and climb and atone. She knew that her people had indeed fallen from the sky, but as victims of a plague called Feather Blight. Today they were known as Gubbings, but once they had been the Skykings or woodpecker folk who had dwelled in Italy and England and built their homes in the branches of kingly oaks. Such facts were recorded in the book of Rejoicing, a forbidden volume which she kept in her chest and guarded as if it were a newly hatched egg.

She loved her husband well, and grieved his death. Now she is lonely, a fact her daughter knows full well; and having once spied Robin bathing in a steam by moonlight, she has fallen unwillingly in love with him.

As a member of Judith's congregation, she suggests the matter of Robin's guilt or innocence be tested by a Trial by Rhyme. Herrick is a master poet and it is upon this that she places her trust. It is not misplaced: he wins.

But the Gubbings will not allow him to return to Dean Church and the outer world, ignorant though he remains of their true nature. They insist that he remain a prisoner. Stella points out that Robin was deceived in her name and asks that he and Nicholas be placed in the custody of those whose names were used to lead them here, and become her prisoners. She points out that they may be able to repair the mill and restore it to its function.

Reluctantly, Judith agrees with her logic and commends them into her care, but when she turns her back Stella feels Judith's stare like a scorpion, and knows that Judith has added to her grievances against her . . .

CHAPTER VII

'I COULD eat a bear' said Robin, apparently forgetting that Artor was in the room. 'It was only a metaphor,' he hurried to add, but not before Artor had given him a melancholy look and retired to his bed beside the cradle. 'What I meant to say was, I'm ravenous. Nicholas and I haven't eaten since supper last night.'

'Then we had water-cress,' Nicholas mumbled.

'I can do better than that,' said Stella, her suspicion confirmed that Robin did not eat as he should, and with Aster's help she planned such a meal as she had once served to Philip on his return from a voyage. A less modest woman would have called it a feast.

The brick oven at the side of the fireplace was already laid with a fire. With the help of a flint box, she lit the faggots and swept their ashes into a copper bucket, and placed a loaf of currant bread and a pork pie on the hot hearth and covered them with the ashes. She knew that the bread was ready to eat when she could tap its bottom and hear a faint rumble; and the pie, when its crust was brown. The wainscot table-chair soon tinkled with pewter posnets and thumped with wooden dishes, and the air was wreathed with a redolence of saffron cakes which, though lost upon Stella, excited her guests to anticipatory sniffings and a remark from Nicholas that he hadn't smelled such a fragrance even in the Devil Tavern of Cambridge.

Happiness entered the room like the spirit of Mother Goose; invisible but tangible; protective and proprietary. 'We're birds of a feather,' thought Stella, echoing an old adage originated by her own people, though later claimed by the English peasants. Aster began the meal by asking Robin to ask a blessing.

'Something special. A poem just for the occasion.'

'But poets need time,' protested Stella.

'Mama, he beat Judith in the Trial by Rhyme, didn't he?'

Robin looked doubtful, then confident. 'Something special. What about a blessing for *you* to ask, not me? I'll teach it to you, though.' They joined hands around the table:

> Here a little child I stand,
> Heaving up my either hand;
> Cold as paddocks though they be,
> Here I lift them up to thee,
> For a benizon to fall
> On our meat, and on us all. Amen.

'I'm nine,' she reminded him, 'though of course I'm little in size. Yes, I think that's worthy of Mother Goose. She's one of our saints, you know. The patron of poets. I especially like the paddocks. I had one when I was young.' In Devonshire, 'paddock' was another name for 'frog'.

And so the meal proceeded from dish to delight to dish. . . . Peas and sparrow grass to keep a big man from running to fat. West Country Tarts to plumpen a peeked boy. Firelight; candles; conversation. ' 'Tis not the food but the content that makes the table's merriment. . . .'

Finishing the last cake, Aster said with a meaningful look at Robin:

'Mama used to serve such meals to my father in Exeter. Her *husband*. You don't eat so well in your vicarage, I expect.'

Robin for once was caught at a loss for words, but Nicholas hurried to agree with Aster. (Tomorrow, Stella thought, I will see to healing his leg.)

'Every man needs a cook, and these days it's more economical to marry one than to hire one. That way, they're always at hand. They can cook and sweep and clean and what-have you whenever you like.'

'Yes,' muttered Robin to Nicholas when Stella busied herself with removing the dishes – he seemed to forget the acuteness of her hearing – 'and they always expect conversation. A man can't get any work done. Sermons, now and then; poetry, never, except to *them*.' He spoke not unkindly but with conviction. Then, when Stella returned to the wainscot table chair and raised the table portion into the back of a chair and settled Robin among its constellation of cushions and sat with Aster and Nicholas on stools, he asked her a question which had nothing at all to do with cooks or wives.

'I still don't understand. The Gubbings are Puritans. But are all Puritans Gubbings?'

'Oh, no. Only a very few. We were the first, though. You see, when those gloomy old missionaries – Augustus and his flock – came from Rome in 597 A.D., they found us a fallen race. Literally. Feather Blight had moulted our feathers and most of them hadn't come back, even to later generations. The Celts had continued to be respectful. Once they had worshipped us as gods. They were still putting us into their stories as kings and queens. But the missionaries took one look at our useless wings and stormed 'fallen angels', and we believed them. We actually believed them, it had been so long since we lost the power of flight. We had angered God, they said. He had thrown us out of heaven along with Lucifer. Thus, they explained our past – flight and Heaven – and our present – Hell on earth. There was only one thing to do, they said. Repent. We listened and repented. We have never ceased repenting even to this day. If a child began to develop a pair of wings which looked as if they might actually carry him aloft, they were clipped and trimmed; he was given a lecture on pride; and soon he was clipping his own wings. For a long time most of us stayed right here in Dartmoor because if we went out into the world, someone might discover what was left of our wings and accuse us of being witches or warlocks and hustle us off to a stake. But we *wanted* to go into the world and spread what we thought to be the word. It is all very well to repent of one's own sins.

It is much more fun to make other people repent of theirs.

'It was during the reign of Elizabeth, bless her, that Judith's grandfather reached an important conclusion: *The first to cry witch is rarely accused of witchcraft.* Let us send missionaries out into a world which is rapidly tumbling back into paganism – why, look at Elizabeth, our so-called virgin queen. No more a virgin than Jezebel! Robe them in black like ourselves. Hide their wings. Stamp the fear of God on their faces. We did just that, and they set up such a cry about sin and the Devil and witches that no one – at least not very often – suspected *them.* You see, they were so sincere. They practiced what they preached. The first thing we knew there were Puritans all over England and even settling colonies in the New World. Now, only about one in a hundred Puritans comes from Dartmoor, though of course in Dean Church the number is much higher.'

'One of these days,' said Robin, 'there's going to be a civil war. I can see the division in my own parish.'

'Yes,' said Stella, 'and I hope the Puritans lose. Meanwhile, you had better keep your eye on the Cobbler and the Seamstress and the Blacksmith and—' She hesitated. Should she mention the worst of the lot?

'But you're not at all like your people. You *glow,*' said Robin.

'At heart I'm Elizabethan like my late husband. And that's why Aster and I drank with you at the Harvest Home. Because you rescued Artor. And because you seemed Elizabethan too.'

'Did you have to come back to Dartmoor?'

'I had Aster to think about. Without Philip it was unthinkable for a mother and daughter like us to remain alone in a city of sailors. As you doubtless know, a woman with even a modicum of looks can't walk down the street without being goosed—'

'Mama, you're being irreverent.'

'Without being pinched or, shall we say, investigated, by a sailor. My wings are small enough for any modest garment to hide. But once you start investigating – well, there was constant threat of discovery.'

'And worse,' said Aster direly. 'Things happen to women, you know, when they don't have husbands to protect them. But Mama, we've talked enough about dismal things. Why don't you play for us? Mama plays beautifully,' she added. 'The last man who asked for her hand in marriage said that she played like an angel before the fall. She sings too.'

'I'm sure our guests would rather talk. I have one of Philip's pipes about the place. And some tobacco, I think, straight from the Colonies. Of course it's ten years old.'

'Stella, please play for us.' It was Robin. 'You have the tiniest hands I ever saw on a woman. I see a music in them sweeter than a nightingale.'

'Very well,' she smiled, acquiescing modestly though with a flush of pleasure. She would play 'Halcyon'. It was a love song as old as her people's history.

She sat at the stool before the clavicytherium. If she had been a vain woman, she would have thought: The firelight kindles my hair, drawn into a knot behind my head, and makes it seem to throb like a flame. My skirt of green velvet; my embroidered petticoat peeping naughtily below its rim; my bare shoulders, their freckles invisible except at close range: even though I wore the same gown when I lived in Exeter with Philip, and now I am thirty and a widow, it is surely more becoming than the white apron and the black pointed cap of a Puritan.

As it was, she thought: I am playing for Robin, and what he sees is less than he deserves but perhaps more than what he has found in Dean Church.

And so she played. The instrument itself was not

powerful. It tinkled sweetly through the room, rather like a harp (though not, she hoped, as insipid as an angel's harp). But when she sang, the room became an orchard, and the treetops trembled with an April of birds. You could hear their wings, you could hear their songs; you could hear their pain at winter's theft, their exultation at the melting ice, the budding boughs, the building of nests.

> *A halcyon is my love,*
> *Who nested on the sea,*
> *But when I flung my cunning net,*
> *My love eluded me.*

> *A halcyon is my love,*
> *Who nested on the sea,*
> *But when I lifted open hands,*
> *My love came down to me.*

She rose from the stool, half apologetic; she had quite forgotten Aster and Nicholas. She had sung only to Robin; she had become her song.

'You must be very tired,' she said. 'Such a day you've had! The Trial—'

But no one was listening to her; looking at her, yes, but not listening to her words. Robin had started to cry. Philip had never cried, not even before his death. Gubbings would rather be locked in the stocks than cry. And yet this big, manly man was crying without shame and not even trying to hide his face or brush the tears with his hand.

She sank to her knees beside his stool. 'Dearest Robin, how have I made you sad?'

'Usually,' he said, almost with reluctance, 'I like my vicarage, I like to hoe in my garden or play Hoodman's Blind with the children. Or preach a sermon even when the congregation goes to sleep and I have to throw my sermon at them. But sometimes I want to walk away to –

otherwhere. A garden with bluebells and sunflowers. Sometimes I gather them in my arms or pile them in wicker arks, and they never wilt. I was there now. Free and yet companioned. Nicholas has already been there with me. But now there were four of us. "But when I lifted open hands. . . ." Isn't it true of the truest love? It flings no nets.'

Lightly she touched his hair. Unlike most of her people, she was not afraid to touch. His hair was thick and heavy and, like the rest of him, thoroughly masculine. She felt as if she were touching sprays of wheat.

'The garden is always there,' she said. 'We've only to climb the stile. But come to bed now. I'll fix a place for you in the upper story. It's cramped with millstones that don't grind, and cluttered with levers and cogs. I use it as a kind of butterie too, where I store my preserves and my butts of wine, my cheeses and my clothes. I don't know what it smells like. Rusty machines or food or both. But tonight it'll have to do. At least it's better than sleeping in the damp and cold under the mill, though I left two coverlits there and stuffed them with hay, in case any Gubbings came snooping about the place.'

'You see,' said Aster, 'you can't sleep in the room with Mama and me because you're not married to us. It makes it terribly inconvenient. I expect you'll catch your death.'

'I could even sleep in a stock,' said Nicholas. He never complained about his leg, but his face looked white and drawn.

'Here, you must drink some of Mama's poppy head syrup. It will help to rest you. Then we must feed Artor.'

The bear had not stirred from beside the cradle since Robin's tactless remark.

'May I give him a saffron cake?' asked Robin.

'Yes,' Aster said doubtfully, 'but watch your hand. He's been known to bite. He bit Judith on her calf when she said that animals haven't any souls.'

'Of course they have souls. I have a pig named Caligula, and I expect to meet him in heaven. If I get there. He sleeps in my trundle when Nicholas isn't visiting.

He extended a cake as a peace offering. Artor pretended to sleep. 'When Nicholas is there, I make a bed for him by the hearth. It's just as comfortable. And the Candlemaker's widow is feeding him while I'm away.'

Artor accepted the cake.

It was almost morning. Aster appeared to be sleeping with the soundness of youth though less with innocence than a kind of blissful anticipation. Robin and Nicholas, so she supposed, were sleeping among the rusted machines in the loft above her head. She had fixed two pallets for them, given them coverlits and a lantern, and promised tomorrow to transform the place into a solar while they were fixing the cogs or scraping rust or doing whatever was needed to make a mill start grinding after nine years of inactivity.

She stepped onto the porch. The first light of dawn had begun to flush the tors. Usually they resembled huge jagged tombstones, but now they were what they had been to her ancestors before the fall, unabashedly phallic; earth's virility yearning to the fruitful sky. The pre-Christian Romans had said, 'No, you have everything backwards. The earth is a mother, not a father; the sky is a god, not a goddess.' The Christian Romans had said, 'Everything is God, the Father; there is no female principle in nature.' And the Christians after the fall of Rome: 'Let's not speak of male *or* female principles. It's quite indelicate. Repent!'

For once she was not naked. The presence of guests, to say nothing of early-risen Gubbings who would watch the mill for indiscretions or, better, a full-fledged sin, required a certain decorum. She was wearing a nightdress which had come to her by way of Philip, who had raided a

Spanish galleon (yes, the Spaniards were good for *some-thing*), a billowy garment of satin and lace which looked as if it were sewn of spendrift and which, having been sewn in a Catholic country, disclosed nothing but intimated much. Aster had remarked when she went to bed, 'What a shame Nicholas and Robin can't see you like this. Why, the way the green sets off your hair, you look almost young!'

Yes, what a shame. This morning the wind was worse than a chilly love, he was a mere eunuch. Robin in the mill and she on the porch. The rarest time of day, the secret time, and she must waste it with her own companionable thoughts.

But of course she had secretly guessed that he would come to join her. In fact, she had willed him to come. As Aster might have said, she had given him the eye, or at least the inclination. Not that she was a witch as Philip had laughed and half believed. But where was the woman, Gubbing or human, without her witchcraft? Last night she had said to Robin, 'I stand on the porch every morning to greet the dawn,' and now she waited for him with assurance that he would come but impatience at his delay.

He trod lightly on his bare feet, but she heard him even as he descended the ladder from the upper story. She did not turn to face him, however, until he stood beside her and she could no longer pretend to be unaware of his presence. He stood so close to her that she felt the heat of his body. Had she the nostrils of a human, she supposed, she would scent the maleness of him, the musky masculinity which Philip, with his usual directness, had told her other women scented on him. Perhaps it was just as well not to be assaulted by yet another sense. She was not a coquette; she was tongue-tied; she was terrified. There was such a thing as a forest fire. In the chill of the dawn, on that unprotected porch, he was clad in a loin-cloth. He might have been a Faun accosting her in the deep woods.

The impudence of the man! Julia, Corinna, all those other giggling rustic girls – perhaps after all he had taken his pleasure with them. A man who flaunted his naked-ness—

'Stella, you old Puritan,' she said to herself. 'You sound like Judith. Disguising desire as disapproval. Philip would have lost patience with you.'

She expected him to chaff with her; to banter and tease and tempt. It was the way of most attractive men; it had been Philip's way when he hoped to bed her without wed-ding her.

He did not chaff. He looked like a little boy about to cry, this big, ruddy, almost naked man who stirred her more than Philip, because Philip had been the sort of man who had never seemed less or more than thirty; it was impossible to imagine him as a child or an old man. Robin, however, in spite of his size, seemed suddenly younger than Aster.

'St-Stella.'

'Yes, Robin.' She realized now that his nakedness was naturalness and not calculation; he did not know his own attraction.

'You saved my life. And Nicholas.'

'I only made it possible for you to save yourself.'

'Stella, why did you save my life?'

'Because I saw you swimming in a stream by moon-light. And I read the poem you left.'

'Oh,' he said, startled. 'I hope you didn't wait until I climbed out on the bank.'

'Yes.'

'Do you think I'm running to fat? Vicars do. They eat a lot of beef.'

'No.'

93

'You weren't disappointed?'

'No.'

'I never saw *you* swimming by moonlight. Do you?'

'No. I stand on my balcony.'

'You mean like now. You look like a green morning glory!'

'No. I mean like you in the stream.'

'Nude?'

'Naked.'

'But that's a splendid thing to do! Why did you change your habit just this morning?'

'Because I have freckles.'

'I like freckles. They make me think of strawberries.'

'Truly, Robin? You don't prefer the milky whiteness of those simple-minded little things in Dean Church?'

'Too much milk turns my stomach.'

'You mean you've seen their milky whiteness?'

'I don't mean anything of the kind. I mean *if* I saw it.'

A silence fell between them. She felt: the next thing I say must be – significant.

Fortunately, there was no need for her to say anything, significant or trivial. He kissed and encompassed her at the same time, and he was much too quick to be graceful or artful; he was sudden, turbulent, and total; and the years did not tremble back to Philip. It was now Robin, tomorrow and tomorrow. She held him and felt as if she were holding a great armful of sunflowers. Why did she think of him in terms of gardens? He was anything but delicate and floral. It's because he's the earth, she thought, its strength without its cruelty. I am the sky, though almost wingless; he is the summer countryside, with its wheatfields and its gardens, its sweet ruggedness and its rough sweetnesses.

'You don't know about me,' she said. 'You haven't seen my wings. They're little and stubby and not tall and billowing as you might suppose.'

'But you aren't a witch. You've already told me so.'

'No.'

'I'm glad. Not that I would mind if you were, except my position would make it difficult for us. A vicar and a witch – raised eyebrows, a drop in church attendance. But it's nice to have you – otherwise. You're not human then, are you? You're better. I knew there was something different about the Gubbings. Something under those dark robes.'

'Not better. Just different. We were once called Sky-kings. Somehow the name turned into Gubbings. I expect the missionaries put "grubbing" into it.' She was not really thinking about the name of her people, however. She was thinking: He spoke as if he intended to take me home with him to Dean Church. To his vicarage. To be a vicar's wife. First, we'll have our own private ceremony before the altar of Picus and Mother Goose, with only Aster and Nicholas for witnesses. He seems to like me in green. Somehow I must manage to get some silk from Exeter, and I will leave an opening for my wings like the brides in the old time, and Aster shall read a passage from the Book of Rejoicing before it became the Book of Redemption. Then, a public wedding in his own church to satisfy *his* conscience. After all, he is a man of God, even if the wrong God.

'I don't know much about my own ancestry,' he was saying. 'Farmers, goldsmiths – possibly a Fawn or two a long way back. Will such a pedestrian lineage do?'

'I suspect you have at least one phoenix in your family tree. Even if you haven't – yes, you'll do, my dear.'

'*Mama, we've got him!*' Aster pranced in the doorway. Her pale little features were flushed with triumph. 'I heard everything. He's going to marry you. Ask him about Nicholas for me.'

'*Marriage?*' It was more a yelp than a question. The sun had risen above the horizon, but the sunflowers looked as if they were ready to wilt.

Book Three: Robin

CHAPTER VIII

CRAMPED among the cogs and gears, and the jars of marmalade sealed with pig's bladder, cold in spite of his coverlit, he had hardly slept all night. Once he had dozed but Nicholas had groaned in his sleep and Robin had pressed his hand and put to rout whatever demons or Gubbings disturbed his dreams. It had been a happy even if uncomfortable wakefulness, however, companioned as if in his secret garden by those he most loved. Nicholas, the son who had come to him late, and come in need. Stella, the woman whose name meant star. If Nicholas lay beside him, it was Stella who possessed the dark above him, her wings tall and unfettered, and she was smiling and leading him by the hand.

'Sweetest love,' she said. 'We have a journey to make.'

'To the moon? To the star where you found your name?'

'Not nearly so far. Just to the next field. See, where the sunflowers are twittering with sparrows.'

'Sparrows are quarrelsome birds.'

'You don't understand them. They're talking, not quarreling.'

'Can Nicholas come too? He limps, you know.'

'Yes, Nicholas can come too, and he won't need his crutches.'

He heard her stirring directly under him. He gave her time to perform whatever rituals of dress began a woman's day; he expected them to be intricate and endless from his experience with certain accessible young women he had known in London. But the room was quiet before she had even had time to preen in a mirror. She must have walked onto the porch. Perhaps at last they could talk without being interrupted or overheard. Forgetting his tunic and sandals, he scrambled down the ladder and, scrupulous not to awaken Aster, stepped onto the porch. He almost fell over the railing in his eagerness to join her. Clumsy Robin! Artor could teach him grace. He had so much wanted to greet her with a pretty speech, a bow from the waist, a courtly gesture: Raleigh to her Elizabeth.

But after the first awkwardness, her beauty – lord, what sinful ankles! – had loosened his tongue ('A sweet disorder in the dress kindles in clothes a wantonness.') And then the confession that she loved him. She, the uncrowned queen, loved this, big, awkward fellow who stumbled over his own feet and who preached in a country parish where farmers thought that Catullus was a new kind of cover crop. It was not the first time a woman had claimed to love him; many women had made such a claim. But he could never forget Anna, his prettiest cousin, saying to him when he was a boy and frantically in love with her, 'Robin, you ought to be a farmer, not a goldsmith. You can make a daisy grow out of a stone, but you can't even put a clasp on a bracelet!' Then she had married his closest friend, who became the best goldsmith in London.

But Stella truly loved him. They would find a way to escape from Dartmoor and go to Dean Church or Exeter or London, or take a voyage to one of those lands of Philip's adventurings. His thoughts reeled in a benign bacchanalia, a banquet of the senses. Stella, the star;

97

Stella, the woman, whose body was Eden without prohibitions even for snakes. Every apple ripe to be plucked!

And then that precocious child had appeared in the door and shouted, 'Mama, we've got him.'

He felt like a stag at bay. Hounds at his hooves, hunters just over the hill. Rescue, asylum, supper, and talk about love: all, all a conspiracy, mother and daughter conspiring together to lure him into their 'cunning net'. Till now, he had not rejected, he had simply ignored, the prospect of marriage. He had seen too many smug little brides dragging big, free-striding boys to the altar because of a night in the hay. He had visited too many cottages where smug little brides turned into shrewish old wives and their husbands turned to ale. There *were* happy marriages. His dead parents were said to have been happy (though his father had jumped out of a window for unaccountable reasons when Robin was an infant). But for every free and blissful union, there were a hundred inquisitorial dungeons. It was the cold legality of the institution which repelled him; the finality, enduring even into Heaven or (Hell?), if one could believe certain unmarried churchmen. The Elizabethan in him cried: 'Love because you will.' His own church, even more the Puritans, cried, 'Love because of sentences – a sentence – imposed by a minister.'

He had been a chaplain and he was now a vicar; he always shuddered when he had to speak those irrevocable words over a callow couple who beamed at each other as if marriage were daffodils and daisies, when it was more likely to be bracken and nettles.

'The sun is up,' said Stella. 'We ought to go in or we'll be seen.' Her skin was so pale that the freckles on her cheeks looked like strawberries floating in milk. He felt a smarting of pity; it was hard for her, being exposed in her connivance. Still, she *had* connived.

98

They walked silently into the houseplace. Last night's joy – where had it gone? Mother Goose had departed, the music had fled from the clavicytherium. The keyboard looked as if it would growl instead of tinkle, and Stella looked as if she would rather sing hymns than 'Halcyons'.

'Bring Nicholas down and I'll fix breakfast. Will moorhen eggs do?'

'Yes, thank you, Stella.'

At breakfast, Nicholas stared from Robin to Stella to Aster, but no one said a word. Finally Aster said darkly, 'Nicholas, your friend turned us down. I expect Mama will have to marry a Gubbing now.'

'See to the dishes, Aster.' (Personally, he would have liked to spank the girl, though he supposed that he ought to be grateful for her warning.) 'I promised Judith a new apron. I'll take it to her this afternoon.' Her voice quavered when she turned to Robin. 'Will you and Nicholas have a look at the machinery? If we don't get the mill to grinding, you may face another trial.'

'I had a look at it last night,' he said. 'The cog wheel is all right except for a little rust. So is the brake wheel. It's the wallowers which is broken. It looks as if the last miller lost his temper and kicked it. I found some spare parts in an old sack, though, and I think you can even grind peas in a day or two. You'll have peas, porridge *and* flour.'

'Forget the peas. Just so we can grind wheat.'

Robin and Nicholas toiled over the machinery for the rest of the morning. The wallowers had to be straightened and oiled, rust had to be chipped from the brake wheel right on down to the stone nuts (which were not made of stone; they got their name because they turned the grinding stones). Most of the time Nicholas sat on the wooden floor and chipped with an iron chisel while Robin bent, replaced, and hammered. Between hammerings, and after a discreet silence, Nicholas asked:

99

'What happened, Robin? You hardly said a word to Stella at breakfast. She looked as if she wanted to cry.'

'Stella wants a husband.'

'You mean she came right out and asked you? But it's for you to do the asking!'

'No, she didn't ask me herself, and it's *not* for me to do the asking, since I don't want a wife. But Aster spoke in behalf of her mother.'

'You might do worse,' said Nicholas. 'I don't much care for moorhen eggs, but that was a fine pork pie last night.'

'I might do worse, but I'm not going to do at all.'

He did not tell Nicholas about Aster's own net. There was no point in terrorizing him when the girl would not be a real menace for several years.

'Well,' said Nicholas cheerfully, 'I guess we can make do on our own.'

'Nicholas, are you disappointed? Did you have your heart set on marrying me off?'

'No,' said Nicholas without hesitation. 'I never really wanted you to marry Stella in the first place. I like her very much. She makes me think of my mother, if my mother hadn't been a Puritan. She's a good cook. And she's the best prospect you've had. But *nobody* is good enough for you. And we would have had to take Aster too. Sometimes I almost get the feeling that little girl has me staked out for herself.' A perceptive boy, Nicholas. 'She has that look about her. Do you know what I mean? Patient and predatory. If she's begun to stalk at nine, you can imagine what she'll be like at fifteen.'

'Thirteen, I would think. They marry young in these parts.'

'God protect us from matrimonial women.'

They chipped and hammered.

It was afternoon. Stella was carrying the finished

apron, 'white as an angel's wing' according to Judith's specifications, and Robin was carrying the first sack of flour from the resurrected mill. They had left Nicholas (wary) and Aster (patient) to prepare dinner.

Half a mile of bracken lay between them and the town of the Gubbings. They followed a tortuous, sometimes sodden path which Stella charitably called the Heath Road. There were daisies among the stalks of bracken, little white moths of bloom among those skeletons. But Robin hardly noticed them; he noticed the skeletons.

'Robin,' said Stella when Nicholas and Aster could no longer hear them. 'I'm sorry about what Aster said on the porch. I never set out to trap you. But I did hope to marry you. From the time we drank together at the Harvest Home. You must try not to blame me too much. You see, my dear, I'm lonely. It's been such a long time since Philip died.'

'Are you, Stella? You seemed so contented with the mill.'

'Oh, sometimes I was. But what is contentment except an absence of sorrow? It isn't happiness. You know that too. Or why do you swim alone in the streams at night?'

'I'm not sure,' he confessed.

'You're looking for something you don't find in your vicarage, in your flock, even with your nieces and nephews and pig. It's the same with me. It's why I stand on the porch in the morning. Nine years, and no one to really talk to except Aster. The Gubbings never say what they mean. I've had my ankles ogled until I wanted to lift my petticoat, lower a stocking, and flash a naked knee! I've even been pinched in the Tabernacle. But do you think they would admit that they want me as anything except a begetter of little Gubbings? They'd as soon let their hair grow as long as the King's. As for the women, Judith used to be my friend, and sometimes we still have chats, but I always feel as if she's hoping to find a wrinkle.'

'She won't find any.'

'Not yet. Soon, though. How does your poem go? I heard that little simpleton, What's-her-name, the one with the outsized bosom, reciting it to a friend while they were gleaning in the fields one day. Of course she said it badly. She sounded like a chicken with the pip. But I do remember a few lines:

> *Gather ye rosebuds while ye may,*
> *Old time is still a-flying . . .'*

Robin took up the verse:

> *and this same flower that smiles today*
> *Tomorrow will be dying.*

'In other words,' she said, 'I fancied you, Robin. And I rather hoped you would consider me a rosebud, even though I had already been gathered once.'

He dropped the sack of flour and tried to make up his mind whether he should shake her or kiss her. He ended by gripping her shoulders – and sniffing her sweetness of lavendar and storax – and feeling the warmth of her hidden wings – and waiting, wanting – more than a vicar should want. Now they had come to a clump of Cornish Heath, its four- and five-pronged leaves punctuated with pink flowers. But he himself felt like a Twisted Heath, beaten by the wind and splattered with mud. It was not the walk which had put him in such a state.

'Oh, Stella, you're so much more than a rosebud. You're a full-blown blossom and I do want to gather you!'

'I know you do,' she said. 'But I also know what you mean by gathering.'

'It's been two years since I bedded a girl,' he said forlornly. 'If *that* isn't forebearance. And it's not as if I haven't had chances.' He *had* had chances, and not just Corinna and Julia and most of their friends. Lady Margaret, resplendent in lace, who rode from her manor house in the country to hear his sermons. The Candlemaker's widow who said that she was tired of making candles. . . .

'I know you have. I rather expected that little simple What's-her-name to gather *you*, she was so brazen. I respect your forebearance with her.'

'Anyway, you weren't going to be like the other women. I was thinking about taking you away to Exeter and finding a cottage for you. A *permanent* cottage.'

'You would have to keep me secret from your parishioners, and I'm not meant to be a secret woman. Do you expect me to be a latter-day Whore of Babylon? I don't want to be kept, I want to be shown. Philip was proud of me.'

'And so am I. We could move to London. I could give up the Church. It isn't what it was, not with all these Puritans like rats in the rafters. I could become a goldsmith like my uncle. You know, I was apprenticed to him for six years.' He did not tell her how many carkanets he had bent or smashed, how many pomander bracelets he had forgotten to spice.

'Robin,' said Stella, 'when a woman has had heaven, do you expect her to settle for limbo?'

'I've been called lots of things, but never limbo. I think I would prefer to be called Hell. At least it's scarlet instead of gray.'

'I didn't mean you were gray. You're like a rainbow. I only meant that having been one man's wife, how can I be another man's woman?'

'I thought you said you were an Elizabethan. Did Elizabeth hesitate to take Essex for a lover? And did her subjects object until he got political aspirations? You don't think they really thought she was a virgin all those years, or wanted her to be? Those were lusty times. Marriage, on the other hand, is like a four-poster bed with the curtains drawn. Depending on your company, it may be cozy, it may be cold, but either way you can't help wondering what's going on outside.'

'I'm lusty, Robin, but I'm not lustful.'

'Well, I'm lusty and lustful too. I want to drag you behind the nearest tor. It's your own fault for looking as if your mother were an angel and your father were a Faun.'

'But Robin, there aren't any female angels. You're a vicar. You ought to know that. They're either male like Gabriel or inbetween.'

A poet does not welcome criticism of his similes – not when he is unsuccessfully attempting seduction.

'And what's so sacred,' he snapped, 'about a few words mumbled by a man no better than I am? I've mumbled them often enough myself, God forgive me. Besides, you aren't even a Christian. I thought that in the old time your people loved freely and merrily and with no sense of sin.'

'It's true. They did. Just like the Fauns and the Dryads the Romans told us about. But I'm not of the old time and not of the new time either. I'm me, Stella, and no one else.'

'You're a Puritan.' He regretted the hateful words as soon as they left his tongue, but she was maddening him to distraction. To look incomparably delectable, even to set the table, then to turn him away from the feast!

'No, I'm not a Puritan. The Puritans think you have to get married in order to have sex, and you shouldn't have sex even when you get married unless you want to beget. I don't say anybody else has to marry. My best friend in Exeter was a harlot. I respected her far more than I respect Judith. Speaking for myself, though, I'll risk the four-poster bed – posters, curtains, and all.'

'Women don't feel as men do, or they wouldn't haggle at a time like this.'

'What do you mean, Robin?'

'I mean I'm on fire!'

'Where, Robin?'

'In the pelvis, where else?'

'But of course women feel the same as men at such a time. My race has always been known for its strong but sensitive pelvises. The way the bones come together, don't you know. Philip said that I had an admirable pelvis. How did he phrase it? Something about a pinnace and a snug harbor. Right now I feel as if there were fireships in my harbor.'

'What are you going to do about them?'

'Let them burn, I suppose, since there doesn't seem to be a bucket at hand.'

'Bell, you mean. Not bucket. Wedding bell.' The obstinacy of the woman! The unmitigated cruelty! All those strawberries hidden in a black robe, till they shriveled and dried into dust. 'Why, Stella, why?'

A Gubbing farmer leaned on his hoe and stared at them with a look between speculation and suspicion. A falcon lumbered out of a thicket of bracken. A gyrfalcon. Such a lordly bird! The first bird of any kind which he had seen in Dartmoor.

'It is the wedding ceremony you want?' he pursued. 'The ritual, the gown, the audience?'

'Yes, I would like a wedding,' she admitted. 'A private one, though, with a few words spoken from the Book of Rejoicing. Simple words, but beautiful. The same as when the Woodpecker God wedded the Lark Goddess. He was quite the popinjay in his youth. But once he married he never strayed from the nest. And yes, I would like to look my best for you in a green gown with a crimson stomacher, and with my wings showing through like flames. You've never seen my wings.'

'No.'

'They're small but they're just the color of my hair. If you like red.'

'Very much.'

'And I want a wedding feast with fermented myrrh and sunflower cakes. I like tradition. I like ceremony, so long as it's a silken robe to be worn lightly and not a wool surplice.'

'And that's why you want to be married?'

'That's only one reason. The least important. I want to be married because it's a way of saying thank you to Picus. Thank you for the harvest, thank you for the vintage, thank you even for earth's white sleep in winter. You see, Robin, the seasons turn but they always return. It's Picus' way of telling us, "What sleeps, awakens, What's lost is found. Whenever you doubt me, ask yourselves a question: Have I ever misplaced an April?" So it all comes down to this. Marriage – and the parenthood which follows – is a way of saying grace to Picus, or to your Christian God, who I suspect is really the same fellow under his feathers. Didn't his only son ascend into heaven? How did he get there unless he flew? Marriage is a grace and a promise never to doubt that the world, however muddled it seems to us at times, runs like a beautifully wrought waterclock (not that abomination in the square).'

'And if I promised always to love you, wouldn't you believe me?'

'I think I would. But marriage is also a way of telling other people you've made the promise.'

'To win their approval?'

'Robin, Robin, I don't give a feather if other people approve of me, except for you and Aster and Nicholas. But everyone who truly marries is proud of his union; he wants to share and affirm with others like himself.'

Robin was silent when she finished her plea. It seemed a profanation to answer her with anything less than a poem or a psalm. It would be a long time before he complained about talkative women – not when they talked like Stella. Now they were approaching the tors which surrounded the town. The afternoon sun touched the dark granite to roseate flickerings. The thought came to Robin that the tors were giant Gubbings in dark surplices; the flickerings were the passions which they could not hide. Love, anger, envy, hate. The actual Gubbings were about their work in the fens which passed for fields – cutting sod, hoeing, mining for tin – but no one was quite close enough to overhear them.

'I think I understand. You're a rare woman, Stella. But I guess I'm afraid of marriage. I guess I'm a coward.'

'Step closer to me, Robin. That falcon we saw – he's directly over us now. He looks as if he might attack you.'

Indeed, the bird seemed poised to drop on his head! His talons looked like hooks, and his beak – well, Robin would have preferred to be stabbed with a dirk.

'But what about you?'

'He seems to fancy me. I think I've seen him before. First at the Harvest Home. Then near the mill.'

'But you said there weren't any birds in Dartmoor.'

'There weren't. And this one is going away. Now, as to what you were saying about your cowardice. No, my dear, you're not a coward. You're already so burdened with love that you hesitate to take on the additional burden of marriage, and for you it would be difficult, even if beautiful, because you take your loves so seriously. You see, Robin, there are some people who love too easily. Every sunset moves them to tears. Every sunrise makes them laugh. They are good and gracious people, but they fall out of love as easily as they fall in. You aren't such a person. You've added love to love without ever subtracting, you've filled the jewel casket of your heart with topaz upon opal upon calcedon without ever misplacing a stone. Your nieces and nephews who come to visit you – Nicholas has told me about them. You love them as if they were your own children. And just in the last few days, you've come to love Nicholas as a friend and little brother and son all at once. You want to heal his leg; you ache when he aches; you think that one more big love will be more aches than you can bear. It will assault you like an Armada, and it won't be scattered by a providential storm.'

'I'm afraid you over rate me, Stella. I'm as fickle as the next man, and a poor excuse for a vicar.'

'You don't fool me with your light, bantering poetry. Oh, it's part of you, a very real part. There's a joy in you as pure as a wheatfield amber in the sun! But I know the solid red earth under the wind-frolicked wheat. The wheat may be harvested but the earth abides. Hush now, Robin. Everybody is looking at us. That old man has been leaning on his hoe for the last five minutes, and you can be sure he isn't thinking about beets. Look stern and dutiful or people will think we've sinned. Or know it. They think it already of every man and woman who smile at each other.'

'We haven't smiled at each other since early morning.'

She pressed his hand. 'I won't burden you with a wife,' she whispered, 'but I will burden you with another friend. May I come next to Nicholas?'

'Goodness,' said Judith erupting from behind a tor like a spurt of black lava. She should have said 'badness', to judge from her face. She was staring a crucifixion at Stella, and staring – dear God, could it be matrimony? – at him. 'You two look positively ashen. Is the mill not working? Or have you something to confess?'

Robin flung the sack of flour at her feet. It burst at the

seams and a fine white powder splattered her gown. She looked at him in angry astonishment.

'I ground it, you bake it,' he snapped, seizing Stella's hand and hurrying her back toward the mill.

CHAPTER IX

SUPPER, unlike breakfast, was not eaten in gloom. There were no intimacies; there was no music; Mother Goose had not returned to bestow a benediction on the household; but there was a charfish as delectable as last night's pork, and there was the shared if unspoken assumption that they were to allow no personal complications, misunderstandings, disappointments to interfere with their plans for escape from Dartmoor. It was difficult; complications threatened even if they did not quite erupt into the conversation. Robin's brain was like a hay stack assaulted by a wind devil: thoughts awhirl, straws in every direction. Was a four-poster bed, even with drawn curtains, not after all superior to a trundle bed? Was Stella a saint or a goddess or merely the most maddeningly desirable woman he had ever met? The sheer fragrance of her excited his heart to pound like a moth trapped in a lantern.

As for Stella, she never once alluded to their confrontation of the morning and their conversation of the afternoon (but why did she have to lean so perilously close to him when she was serving the bread? Why did she have to wear another gown from Exeter, its skirt fashionably opened in front to reveal a kirtle embroidered with a nest and green intertwining branches?). She treated him with the familiar affection of a sister (but why did she flash her ankles whenever she crossed the room?). She talked about tin-mining in the tors. 'The Gubbings use tin for their crucifixes – the little ones they place above their doors.' She talked about baking bread. 'I learned how to bake from my friend, the harlot. You remember.' (Yes, he remembered). 'A scattering of pumpkin seeds never hurts.' But the music of her voice alchemized the tin and turned the bread into cake.

Nicholas was no help when he asked: 'Aren't pumpkin seeds an aphrodisiac? I read that in some Latin author, I believe. The Roman emperors never liked to give up, you know.'

'Aphrodisiacs, did you say? I wondered why the Gubbing men seem to relish my bread.'

'Am I intruding?'

Someone had entered the room. No one had heard her climb the stairs; she had not even knocked; she had simply materialized as silently as a shadow. Now she stood in the doorway, stern and solidified, until entry became possession.

It was Judith.

It was Eris, goddess of discord. When the gods excluded her from the wedding of Thetis and Peleus, she showed such 'suspicion, discontent, and strife' that the whole Hellenic world exploded into the Trojan War. If Judith could not begin a war, she could arrange a masterful crucifixion.

'I knocked on the door,' she said, 'but you must not have heard me. You were talking about aphrodisiacs, I believe, and Stella was revealing one of her culinary secrets.' She evaluated the room with a woman's ability to note a hundred details in one rapid and all-inclusive look.

'So this is what you've done to the mill. I must say you've shown a taste for Sybaritic luxury.' She noted the wainscot table-chair, the trundle bed with its coverlit like a rich tapestry of Skykings wheeling among the clouds, the cushioned stools, particularly the clavicytherium. 'I understand that our late and unlamented Elizabeth used to play that instrument.'

'It sounds like a harp,' said Robin.

'Oh? Of course I've never heard a clavicytherium, but I should imagine it would sound like one of those harps which fell out of heaven with Lucifer and our own unfortunate ancestors. Melodious but warped. And this is the bread you were discussing.' She pointed to the loaf as if it were a stone phallus.

'Yes,' said Aster. 'Nicholas told us about the pumpkin seeds being aphrodisiacs. He's very clever. He read it in a Latin author.' Aster's knowledge of aphrodisiacs was limited. Probably she confused them with the diet of the goddess Aphrodite. But Judith winced as if the child had said 'orgy' or 'Priapus'.

'Indeed! You may give me a portion of fish, but I will forego the bread.'

A silence fell on the table, and Judith filled it – captured it, one might say – with the avidity of an eagle pouncing on a lark.

'You know, Master Herrick, Stella and I are exactly the same age. We were friends together before her sojourn in Exeter.' She made the sojourn in Exeter sound like a visit to the fleshpots of Babylon.

'She told me,' said Robin stoutly. 'I understand her late husband Philip voyaged as far as Virginia and Massachusetts. It was men like him who made it possible to found the colony at Plymouth.' That should silence her. After all, Plymouth was notoriously Puritan.

But Judith did not choose to pursue the subject of voyages and colonies. 'Before she left for Exeter, we both received offers of matrimony from upstanding young Gubbings. She declined for the sake of adventure, I for the sake of the church. But then, Robin' – it was the first time that she had used his given name, and in speaking to him now she seemed to exclude everyone else in the room – 'you have made a similar renunciation, haven't you?'

'Yes,' he admitted, 'though less complete than your own.'

'Don't belittle yourself,' she continued. 'However we differ in our views, we both serve a church and we both have renounced freedom, adventure, matrimony, and parenthood.'

'You didn't have to renounce a husband,' said Aster. 'Or weren't you asked?'

'But we never regret our sacrifice, our renunciation, do we, Robin?' she continued, as if Aster were no more animate than a table or a stool.

'No, Mistress Judith.' Something was happening to him. Unwelcome but not uncommon. He feared her for Stella's sake; he feared her because she would turn on him and Nicholas at the first hint of escape. But he had learned to respect her during the Trial by Rhyme and now he was beginning to pity her. It was not because she was flattering him at the expense of his friends; it was because she felt the need to flatter him; to flirt in her fumbling, Puritan way; it was because he recognized her need, denied, thwarted, but pathetically feminine and, in spite of her wings, human. Oh, she was not to be compared with Stella. Even if she had gone to Exeter and found a husband, she might have turned into a nag and a scold. But she was a woman with not a little beauty lingering under her robe – you could tell as much from her ankles – you could tell a lot about a woman from her ankles. Her heart was twisted like wind-battered bracken, but perhaps there were daisies among the skeletal stalks. Like most men, he thought that there was nothing sadder than an aging virgin.

Fortunately, she soon alarmed him into forgetting his pity.

'Well, I shan't stay for dessert, though I expect you're having one of those dishes they serve in the taverns of Exeter. A West Country tart, no doubt. Judging from your furnishings and your table fare, Stella, *one would almost think that you had been to court.*' Such a comment, delivered with a gracious smile, might have been a compliment in London. Coming from a king-despising Puritan in Dartmoor, it was the ultimate condemnation. No, she managed a further thrust. 'The court of Elizabeth, the bitch queen, not our bumbling Charles. You needn't see me to the door, Robin.' He had not intended to see her to the door. He had been too angry in behalf of Stella. 'We shall meet again very soon, I expect.'

Stella sighed when Judith had left the mill. If her wings had been visible and had they been long and willowy as he imagined, instead of short and stubby as Stella claimed, he supposed that they would be dragging the floor.

'She has grounds for a new trial.'

'What have we done?'

'For one thing, you and Nicholas are supposed to be my apprentices, and since you're male, I'm supposed to feed you under the mill, not in it. I have no doubt she poked around down there and decided you're sleeping in the upper story, if not in this very room.'

'But we left some blankets and coverlits.'

'And forgot to rumple them.'

'Is that all?'

'It's quite enough. But she is also the first Gubbing ever to see the interior of this mill since I came to occupy it. This room, The Book of Redemption doesn't treat such matters specifically. But it reads: "Live with the sweet frugality of the blackbird, who flaunts no plumage, neither of self nor nest." In the Book of Rejoicing, of course, the passage refers to a priest, not a layman, and it continues, "But compensates by disporting with his mate in amorous and uncaged delight." But the censors saw to that.'

'And to Judith, we must seem to be living more like pheasants than blackbirds.'

'Exactly.'

'But you're a queen, Stella. She can't touch you and Aster, can she?'

'If there are fallen angels, there must be fallen queens. She can always give me a push. If anyone is safe, I think it must be you. Provided you take the necessary measures.'

'Me?' Somehow she made 'measures' sound like 'antidotes', a draft of hemlock, a pinch of wolfsbane.

'It was the way she looked at you.'

'As if she would like to save my soul?'

'Your body.'

'It's a good thing she didn't see him naked in the moonlight,' interjected Aster.

'She saw enough. Her imagination is very vivid. I remember as a girl she would point out a Gubbing boy and say to me: "His plumage is russet – must prettier than his beet-red hair" or "His wings have points as sharp as spears" or "He's as naked as a human – not a feather anywhere!" She didn't need to see, she imagined, and once we *did* see, you might say we peeped, and she was right, he was naked as a human. You can be sure, Robin, that she knows what you look like from your golden hair right on down to your pelvis. As much as *I* know.'

'What are we going to do?'

'Do? Why, escape from Dartmoor, what else?' She did not try to hide her excitement. She must have had such a look when she walked to Exeter as a girl. She looked like a fallen angel about to recover the power of flight.

Robin deliberated. Escape from Dartmoor. Stella and Aster exposed to a hostile world. Either they must continue to dress and perform like Puritans to avert suspicion, or they must dress as became their femininity and risk exposure as witches. Stella's beauty, unsheathed, would make her particularly vulnerable. Men would like an excuse to fondle and undress her, and while she could no doubt resist the undressing, an impertinent hand might stray to her wings, and then the damning cry, 'A witch, a witch!'

'It's all my fault,' said Robin. 'If I hadn't come blundering in here with Nicholas, you could have gone right on living in your mill.'

'You didn't blunder, you were lured. If we only get you safely out of the place, I'll be eternally grateful. I'll offer a basket of acorns to Picus.'

'And I'll say a prayer to Mother Goose,' said Aster, looking at Nicholas as if they had already plighted their troth.

'In the autumn,' said Stella, 'the cuckoos migrate to Africa. We can do without their song through the winter. But oh, when they return in spring! It's enough to make you cry.' (They had made Robin cry as late as the summer. Had she noticed his tears the night when he bathed in the stream?) 'You think you brought me danger. Perhaps you did. But I would rather be an eagle beleagured by a storm than a fledgling which never left the nest. And I believe Aster feels the same way.'

'Oh, yes.' (Looking at Nicholas.) 'Beleaguer me all you like.'

'Before we escape,' said Stella, 'we must look to Nicholas' leg. It hurts me to see him limp, and I suspect I have just the remedy. The Gubbings bring their children to me in the Tabernacle and I've had considerable success with certain remedies suggested in the Book of Rejoicing. I've even helped the mothers with a difficult lay or hatch. In Dean Church, I expect, they would think I had learned my skills from Satan.' She settled him in the trundle and procceded to open the tall-legged chest, which contained an assortment of fragrant vials and jars.

Aster scurried across the room to hold Nicholas' hand.

'Why don't you wash the supper dishes for your mother?' he suggested.

'Would you like a stiff drink of ale?'

'No. Not if Robin will sit by me.'

Six years could not have dragged Robin from Nicholas' side. He would have broken his own leg to free the boy from this crutches.

Aster tackled the dishes with a glare which would have done credit to Judith and set up a clatter of wood and pewter.

'And we can plan our escape while you're working on my knee,' said Nicholas.

'It's a simple enough remedy,' said Stella. 'You've drunk rose-tip wine, haven't you? Well, you simply mix it with juice from the flowers of the Angels Trumpet Tree and a dash of Devil's Wort – I rather like the symbolism – and massage it into the skin. You have to massage briskly and hard. Manipulate too. It has to penetrate all the way to the bone. And then it's a few days before you start to show any improvement. By the way, you've been very well treated up to now. I can see the handiwork of a skilful apothecary. The swelling is gone. There's little redness. All I have to do is complete what he began. Was it your father?'

'It was Robin.'

'I should have known it wasn't your father.' She began to massage his leg with unerring but necessarily hurtful hands. When Nicholas winced, she bent and kissed him on the cheek. 'You're very brave. You haven't cried out once. Do, if you like.'

'I don't need to,' he said. 'Not with you and Robin here.'

Stella's concern for the boy was as evident in her face as in her fingers, and Robin watched her less with desire than with adoration. He would have liked to put her in a shrine and kneel to her. He would have liked to bring her offerings of acorns and sunflowers. He was not ashamed that he had wanted her as his woman and not his wife. But at least for the moment his feelings were altogether bodiless. A woman like Stella, an infinite woman, could awake an infinity of responses in a man. Whether you worshipped Picus or the Christian god, you had to admit (unless you were a Puritan) that a desirable body was meant to be desired. An admirable spirit was meant to be admired.

'The Gubbings patrol the moors,' she said. 'At night with lanterns and pikes. Will-o-the-Wisps, you call them in Dean Church, and they are quite as dangerous as you imagine. By day they are careful not to be seen by outsiders, but there are just as many of them, and their pikes are just as deadly. Anyone who gets past them does so because they let him. Like you and Nicholas. Now they won't let you. With a reasonable excuse, Aster and I can come and go as we choose. But only until Judith brings charges against us in the Tabernacle. She will probably wait until the town meeting tomorrow afternoon. So we still have a little time to make our plans.

'If we can only get to Dean Church,' said Robin. 'I know there are Gubbings in the village, and Puritans who aren't Gubbings like Nicholas' parents. But mostly there are good old Anglicans. We can get some horses and ride to Exeter. Take ship to France, if we like. I have a little money left to me by my mother.'

'What about this?' said Stella. 'Aster and I will manage to lose Artor again and prod him in the direction of Dean Church. We'll meet you in the field where they held the Harvest Home and then make further plans. But first there's the matter of Judith. You and Nicholas can't get out of Dartmoor except with her help.'

'I don't dislike the woman,' said Robin, 'But she reminds me of the neighbor's cat who ate my pet sparrow, Phil. She was only doing what comes natural to cats, but I always felt uncomfortable with her after that. I feel the same way with Judith. If she were simply wicked, I would know where I stood with her.'

'She isn't simply anything, she's a very complicated woman. Do you pity her, Robin?'

'When I remember what she was, yes. A kitten instead of a cat. Milk before it has turned sour. But I fear her too. Knowing what she's missed, there's no telling what she might do. Kittens grow claws. Sour milk turns the stomach.'

'But that's the point. You must make her remember what she's missed. You must make her wonder if just possibly she might still get it – and more.'

'I don't understand.' He understood perfectly. 'Get what?'

'You. You'll have to sweet-talk her into trusting you.'

'*Allure* her,' put in Aster.

'And use her in your escape.'

It went against his grain, using a woman; worse, using his masculinity against her. It downright disgusted him. 'In other words I'm to be a—'

'Seducer,' said Stella. 'You won't actually have to seduce. But you must – well, be your natural charming self. Flatter her a bit. Compliment her hymns. Better yet, compliment her beauty. Gubbings aren't supposed to be vain, but Judith is as proud of her ankles as a London trollop. Let her do the rest, and she *will*, I promise. I've seen her look at you. Remember,' she added, 'four lives are at stake. Have you ever seen a crucifixion?'

'I've seen witches burned at the stake.'

'Crucifixion hurts less but it hurts longer. Or so I'm told.'

'Very well then,' he sighed. 'I'll do my best to flatter her, though her hymns are execrable.'

'You're sure Robin won't actually have to – er—?' Nicholas stammered.

'Reasonably sure,' said Stella. 'But Judith is a beautiful and demanding woman. If it comes to that—'

Robin refused to complete the sentence for her. It seemed to him that he was about to embark upon the unmanliest escape in the history of Christendom.

'Robin, to save you and Nicholas and Aster I would willingly give myself to any Gubbing in Dartmoor, even to that horrid little Miller whose face looks like a wormy beet. A body is flesh and bones and feathers, nothing more. Call it the cottage of the soul if you will, but I still maintain that you can muddy the cottage without muddying the soul; burn it without burning the soul.'

The damnable practicality of the woman! But he had to admit that she was right; he, the male, the sentimentalist, was wrong. He could not afford a show of masculine pride.

'All right, Stella. But I've grown fond of my cottage, and fonder of yours, which incidentally is more like a manor house. Let's hope there are no invasions.'

CHAPTER X

ALL of the sod-built houses of Dartmoor looked more or less identical: severe, vineless, cylindrical, rather as if a large black bird with little imagination had built them to house her eggs and then upended them. Judith's house appeared to have been built by the least imaginative bird, and to hold not even colorless eggs.

The one-room interior, however, did not match the bleak exterior; in fact, it was a distinct surprise. The sod was faced with earthenware tiles; there was a cleanliness which was more than merely cold and a neatness which was more than merely circumspect, and an indefinable something which could only be called taste. It was true that you had to search. The wooden stools were not upholstered with velvet. The bed, heavy with a black quilt, possessed neither a canopy nor a trundle. There was a chest of unpainted, uncarved oak which looked rather like a big chunk of wood that a forester, not a carpenter, had hewn and lost.

But – and herein lay the surprise – there was a wicker cage inhabited by a lark. Robin would have expected a crow, but no, it was a lark. He did not look joyful, but then he looked as joyful as any bird in any cage; that is to say, resigned. Certainly he was well supplied with water (in a thimble) and with sunflower seeds (in a snuff box). It seemed to Robin that the bird typified its mistress. Judith feared beauty; if she included it in her house, she enclosed it in a cage, just as she caged her own body. But the beauty was undeniable. He felt the urge to start opening cages. But alas, he had come to close them.

'Mistress Judith,' he said when she greeted them at the door. 'Nicholas and I would like to ask a favor.'

'I knew you were coming,' she said. 'My people alerted me soon after you left the mill. I rather expected Stella. After what I saw last night, I expected her to presume on our former friendship and—'

He saw that he must choose his words with speed and discretion. The crucifix at her throat, reflected ominously in her eyes.

'We want you to show us around Dartmoor. We want to see how you farm and mine tin.' He did not add: And patrol the area against invaders. 'In short, if we're going to live here, we want to know the place and make ourselves useful.'

'I should think you would find your hands full at the mill. What with repairing machinery and grinding flour – and dining with your mistress in the evening.' She managed to give to 'Mistress' the connotation of 'strumpet'.

'The machinery is running smoothly and we've ground all the wheat your farmers have brought us.' The Gubbings were clumsy farmers. In their lighter moods (so Stella had told him), that is to say, when the stocks were full, they joked among themselves that they had a 'black thumb'. 'Until they bring us more, we have nothing to do. As your Book of Redemption says, the Devil finds work for idle wings.' He had hurriedly scanned the book before his visit and, being a vicar, memorized some verses.

'The word is "hands", not "wings".' (He recalled with dismay that he had confused the version in the Book of Redemption with that in the Book of Rejoicing.) 'And couldn't your mistress find you work preparing the meals you share with her? All those lavish preparations. And such serving vessels I never saw! No earthenware for Stella. Silver pots and spoons!'

'Pewter. No, we're dining very simply today. Water cress and clap bread, I understand. *Under* the mill. As for our supper last night, it was an act of Christian charity for Mistress Stella to invite us to her table. Our sleeping quarters are so damp and chilly that Nicholas' knee began to pain him. He was positively shaking from the cold when she asked us into the mill. As for any impropriety – well, I *am* a vicar. I dine from time to time with most of my parishioners. I should have thought that I proved my integrity at the Trial by Rhyme.'

She did not question the Trial. He knew that she only

half believed him, but he also knew – and this was not vanity, this was the doubt, the question, the hope in her usually impassive face – that she wanted to believe him.

'Why didn't you ask your benefactress to show you about Dartmoor?'

'To start with, she was sewing a robe for you. She said as long as you had a new apron, you should have a robe to go with it. Then Artor ran off again, Aster ran after him, and Stella has gone to look for both of them. She's afraid that Aster will wander into Dean Church and get into trouble.'

'Aster, I should think, could hold her own with a drunken Spaniard. In case you hadn't noticed, she's rather precocious.' (Yes, he had noticed. Give her a few more years, and Lord protect the Spaniard.) 'Well, we shall leave them to their own devices. Stella has privileges.'

'Will you show us about the town and the tors then?'

'First you must have some cowslip tea,' she said in a tone between an invitation and a question. She was still uncertain about his intentions. However, as Robin had observed from the time he had been apprenticed to his uncle, the goldsmith, an attractive woman's capacity for self-deception was as deep as Lucifer's fall into Hell.

'But aren't we taking up your time?'

'I was reading the third chapter in the Book of Redemption. In those days they drowned heretics. So much less satisfactory than burning or crucifixion. Crucifixion has the advantage of giving the sinner time to repent. Burning has the advantage of disposing of the body. But then I know the book by heart anyway, so you weren't interrupting.'

They sat on the hard stools. Nicholas struggled to arrange his leg into a comfortable position.

'Perhaps Nicholas could sit on your bed.' It was a bold

suggestion; it was perhaps a mistake. 'He's very neat. He won't muss the quilt.'

She looked surprised; then she looked at Nicholas to gauge the degree of his discomfort and the cleanliness of his garments. Stella had washed them while he slept and dried them at her hearth, the tall white stickings, the bulging trousers of cheap serge, the muffling coat and the flat, wide-brimmed hat which he held in his hand.

'Here,' she said, drawing him to his feet. 'Take off those boots and stretch full length.' Carefully she arranged a pillow under his head. Her movements, though stiff and unpracticed, were almost maternal. Robin wondered at the color of her hair beneath the cap which she wore even in her house. It had once been red, but was it still a flame like Stella's or had it fallen to embers or even ashes?

'Nicholas is like a son to me,' Robin said. 'Do you know, he helped me to write one of my sermons. His Latin is better than mine.'

'A knowledge of Latin is mandatory among the Gubbings. This so-called King James Bible is a desecration. The translators were poets, not men of God. To turn a pretty phrase, they thought nothing of perverting God's word. Then, too, there are franknesses in the English which the Latin softens. For that matter, I know Greek too. But Latin suffices. Nicholas, I take it you know your Aenied? There are presentiments of Christianity in almost every book.'

'Yes, Mistress Judith.' He promptly quoted from the passage about Aeneas' descent into Hell.

'Splendid. Our Gubbing boys are not so advanced.' She hesitated and seemed to grope for words. 'Before your trial, it's possible I was a trifle outspoken. One sometimes is, in the service of the Lord. There are so many heretics about. David and Jonathan you called yourselves. Yes, an appropriate comparison.'

There were times when Judith looked almost as young as Stella. He was certain that she had never been entirely guileless, not even as a girl. But at least she did not, at this particular moment, look guileful. He was getting a taste of the milk before it had curdled.

Judith kindled a tiny fire on the hearth – she was not one to waste faggots – and heated some water for the tea in a pewter kettle. The lark sang a few bedraggled notes and buried his beak among the sunflower seeds.

'Really, he has a lovely voice,' she said. 'I've taught him several hymns.' Splattering a few drops on the reed rug, she poured the tea into earthenware cups and passed them to her guests.

'The kettle,' she hurried to explain, 'is one which was brought to me by a Gubbing who had just returned from London. We use tin or earthenware locally, of course. Pewter is so – luxurious. But I accepted for fear of hurting his feelings.' Robin observed that she had polished the pewter to a high gloss and that her fingers lingered on the warm metal with obvious delight.

Then she said in a conspiratorial whisper, 'And would you like some honey in your tea?'

'Very much.'

'A wicked luxury, I know. But I have my own hive. The bees came to me of their own accord.' She seemed to take pride in having attracted them. 'They're such industrious creatures, it wouldn't have done to send them away, would it? I find a lesson in the orderliness of the hive.'

'I have a hive in the Vicarage garden. I use honey in my tea, too.'

'Do you, Robin?' She spoke his given name for the first time, as if to reward him because they had found a common interest or, so she implied, an uncommon interest.

'And now,' she said, dutiful again – well, perhaps half

dutiful – 'we've delayed long enough over our tea. You asked me to show you around the tors. Is Nicholas up to the walk?' She usually spoke of him in the third person. Puritans expected their children and young people to act like adults, and yet they treated them like children until they married.

But Nicholas answered for himself. 'Oh, yes. You'd be surprised how fast I can get around. Stella applied a potion.'

'Stella is noted for her potions. There are those who say she used one of a different kind to snare her husband. Personally, I discount the tale. As a girl, she was not uncomely.'

They began their tour. The tors by daylight had a fascination, a grotesquerie, almost amounting to beauty. They seemed to be men and beasts or beast-men turned to stone. This one rising into the antlers of a stag, that one seeming to lift its handless arms in supplication. Here a Griffin with wind-pentangled wings, there a Shellycoat, a Bogle, a Merrow. It was, after all, a place of magic, but locked in a sleep so deep and dreamless that even the pipes of Pan would echo uselessly from tor to tor.

The Gubbings had not dug the original mines; the Celts had dug them along with building stone forts, now in ruin, and burial cairns. The Gubbings, once they lost their power of flight and migrated here from their eastern forests, had reopened and extended the tunnels and, armed only with picks and wheelbarrows, become unwilling miners. Perhaps it was for their mining that they had received their new name from the missionaires. Sky-kings burrowing like moles. Grubbing in the earth. He wondered how many of them besides Stella remembered the sky. Judith for one. In her smoky green eyes, there were yearnings as well as angers.

If the Gubbings were barely adequate as miners, they

were admittedly inadequate as farmers. You would almost think that they had learned their methods from reading Hesiod's Book of Days. A square of tin attached to a shepherd's staff sufficed them for a hoe. Their scythes – and they were belatedly harvesting the wheat which the farmers of Dean Church had already harvested in their own fields – looked as if they had not been sharpened for at least a hundred years. The only beasts of burden were occasional overburdened mules.

'We find them much superior to other animals.'

'How do you mean?'

'For one thing, more reliable. They give their full attention to their work – they are not distracted by, shall we say, the calls of the flesh.'

'You meant they don't mate?' asked Nicholas.

'And there, do you see what that man is holding in his hand?'

'A beet, I believe.'

'Precisely. Root crops are our special pride. Beets, radishes, carrots, and such. As we say in Dartmoor, "a Beet a day keeps the Devil away".'

'I've never seen such a large, firm vegetable,' Robin remarked, trying to ignore the worms.

Gray, gray, everything gray, Robin had thought when they began their explorations. But as imperceptibly as the red tendrils of dawn climbing a hill, the countryside and its people began to show glints of color. First a violet lodging among bracken; then a butterfly fluttering like a tiny spray of wheat which had taken flight; and then a girl and boy giggling behind a tor and holding hands until Judith surprised them with a surprisingly indulgent smile.

'Priscilla and James. Haven't you better work for your hands?'

They nodded nervously and picked up their hoes, but Judith whispered to Robin,

'They're affianced to each other. So one may indulge an occasional intimacy. Don't you agree?'

'I certainly do. They'll hoe better for it.'

She fell silent and looked as if she might be envisioning intimacies, nuptial no doubt, with him. Unmarried women of thirty, he had noticed, rich or poor, English, Spanish, French, and probably Indian, shared a common and unshakable compulsion to wed. He began to long for a return to gray.

'And over there, Judith. May we see that field?' Ostensibly the guided, Robin was actually guiding them toward the borders of Dartmoor. A pointed finger, a question, and Judith was quick to oblige him with answers or demonstrations. They passed farmers and miners. They passed the guards, stern in black and wielding staffs which could batter the brains out of a wolf. But everyone had a smile for Judith – a trifle forced perhaps, a trifle hesitant, but still a smile – and Judith complimented this man's radishes, that man's barrow of tin.

'Joseph, what a sturdy staff. You might have wrestled it from Jacob.'

'I hewed it myself from an oak at the edge of the moors. Good for cracking a Papist's skull, eh?'

'Michael, are you true to your Biblical name?'

'No one gets by *me*. I sent a little boy scurrying back to Dean Church just this morning. He took me for a Bogle.'

'And that field over there behind the tor?' (In Dartmoor, half an acre passed for a field.) 'What do you grow there?' His vision was acute; he could see with perfect clarity that the crop was clover. He also knew that they had come to the edge of Dartmoor.

'Clover for our mules. On the other side there's a waste of bog and fern, and then you come to the farm of a man named Jacob. A good church goer, as you've no doubt observed, but not one of us.'

'I had a mule before I came to Dean Church. He died of mysterious causes. An apothecary said I might have mixed some hen bane in the clover I fed him. They often grow together, don't they?'

'Oh, we're careful to keep it weeded out of *our* clover,' she said. 'Come, let me show you. We prize it next to our beets.' There were no more guards between them and the 'waste of bog and fern'.

Judith fell to her knees and scooped a handful of rich, red earth, which she ran lovingly through her fingers.

'This used to be nothing but a bog. But we trooped out of Dartmoor by night with wheelbarrows and came back with good soil. It must have taken us a month of such trips, and we wore out thirty or more wheels. But isn't it lovely?' She would have made an excellent farmer's wife if she had not been a Judge. There was an earth-love in her. He had to remind himself that there were more hatreds than loves.

When she rose to her feet, he deftly stepped behind her and pinned her in his arms with an inflexible grip, while Nicholas stuffed her mouth with her own handkerchief and bound her hands and feet with strips of cloth recently torn from one of Stella's coverlits. He felt the surprising smallness of her bones, the bulge of her wings against his chest. At first she was too surprised to struggle. Then she seemed – disillusioned? No, disheartened. The heart had gone out of her. She did not even stiffen her wings against him.

'Judith,' he said. 'Forgive me. But we can't stay in Dartmoor, Nicholas and I. You must understand that. For better or worse, I'm a vicar and an Anglican and a loyal subject of the King. And Nicholas' parents must be beside themselves with worry over his disappearance.' Now she had turned to granite in his arms; mute and cold.

'Your guards will find you. Even if they don't you can work yourself free in time.'

Nicholas tugged at his arm. 'Robin, hurry, or they'll find us!'

Robin deposited her on the ground and rested her head on a pillow of clover. She looked so small and defenseless! Hard, implacable Judith who had meant to crucify him! But he felt no hardness toward her.

He had seen her lark.

'Judith, men have loved you. I'm sure of that.' He knelt beside her and kissed her cheek. 'They will again. Let them.'

'Robin, hurry! Stella will think we've been caught.'

'I'm coming, Nicholas.'

As he turned to follow his friend, she managed to work the handkerchief out of her mouth.

'Sodomites!' she spat.

He replaced the gag before she could scream for help. 'You shouldn't have said that, Judith.' But he was glad; she had released him from the burden of pity.

'Let's find Stella.'

Stella was waiting for them in the field of the Harvest Home. He opened his arms to her and closed them around a warmth which did not burn, a wonder of sun-warmed roses. Aster and Artor were with her.

'Are we safe?' she whispered.

'Look,' he said. 'It's the falcon again.'

'I think,' she said, 'that he's trying to warn us.'

Book Four: Stella

CHAPTER XI

EXCEPT for Nicholas' leg, they would have headed for
Exeter on foot and hoped that they were not overtaken by
Gubbings and a wrathful Judith. It was unthinkable to
show themselves in the village. People would question
Robin and Nicholas. Where had they been for the last
three days? Who was this woman with a child and bear,
spied briefly at the Harvest Home and now, apparently, a
part of the Vicar's questionable retinue? In the end, the
whole town would know that they had been to Dartmoor.
Then, the inevitable conclusion that Stella and her
daughter were Gubbings, that the Vicar was, as his
enemies had charged, in league with them, and that justice must proceed swiftly to the stake.

But there was Nicholas' leg.

'We'll hide here in the fields till nightfall,' said Robin.
'Then I'll go to my house and get some pounds and a little
food, and borrow two horses from the Blacksmith's stable.
He's hard of hearing and won't miss them till morning
of course I'll leave him payment – and we shall ride to
Exeter, two to a horse. and make our plans on the way.'

Robin glittered with martial fervor. He might have
been wearing a plume and cuirass. He might have been a
cavalier instead of a vicar; Sir Philip Sidney, poet and
warrior, ready to march against Spain. But great warriors
are greatly loved; they exact suffering from the women

who love them, and Stella suffered for Robin because he had forgotten their danger in the flush of their success. A humble man, he was not used to adventures, flights, escapes. That very morning it was she who had sipped the intoxicating ales of success; it was she who had thought that all the pikes of Dartmoor could not keep them from Exeter. But escape had been too easy. There was still Judith, gargoyle-menacing, behind them.

'Stella, what's the matter? You look as if you had lost your wings.'

'I might as well have lost them a long time ago,' she said. 'I told you they're short and stubby. They wouldn't lift a plump butterfly.'

'You know what I mean. You look as if you don't expect to see me again.'

'I expect to see you, Robin.' She did not say what she feared: in Dartmoor. In the Tabernacle. 'But Judith—'

'Even if she's managed to free herself, she's not going to march after us with all her Gubbings, now, is she Everyone would see them for what they are. They would lose their mystery and terror.'

But don't you see, she wanted to cry, they *can* be mysterious, they *can* be terrible. I saw them crucify a woman because she was caught in adultery, and stone the man.

'We don't know what she might do. She isn't a simple person.'

'I know,' he said with a touch of rue. 'But she isn't a demon either. And she doesn't worship the Devil.'

'Doesn't she?'

'Not knowingly, anyway. I promise you, Stella, you'll see me again, and with the horses.'

'When we start for Exeter, I'll ride behind Robin,' said Nicholas before Aster could suggest another arrangement.

'I suppose I'll ride with Mama,' said Aster with resignation.

Stella had to admit that it was the only sensible plan; dangerous, yes. But then there was no safe plan.

'Come back, Robin,' she said, and followed him with her eyes until he was out of sight, and with her ears until his footsteps were no louder than the creeping of an ant.

Huddled among a copse of hawthorne beside the very stream where Robin had swum in the moon, they waited for dusk to overtake the stubbled fields, the low trees, clustering now with small, apple-like fruits. (May Trees, they were sometimes called. That hateful Puritan ship, the *Mayflower*, its captain a Gubbing, had been named for them.)

Fortunately for the hidden, tonight's moon was a thin curved dragonfly and not a bird of fire. No cuckoos sang in the trees along the river bank. Artor, curling his paws beneath his head, had fallen into a blissful sleep and started to dream about honey trees or female bears with tails like puffballs. The stream lay dusky in the deeper dusk of earth. A sudden breeze blew from the direction of Dartmoor. Stella and Aster were fortified against the cold by their body heat, but Nicholas began to shiver as if he had the ague.

Stella, sitting between him and Aster, encircled each of them with a maternal and protective arm. There was a gentle sweetness in holding Nicholas; she felt united with Robin in loving him. She felt the smallness of his bones, the narrowness of his shoulders; not in the least feminine, though; trim and stoutly knit as became his people.

'Here,' she said. 'I have enough heat for both of us.'

'I'm not cold.'

'No. I'd forgotten.'

'Forgotten what?'

'That you don't get cold like Robin. But you're still shivering.'

'My leg hurts a bit.'

'It will for some time. But it's getting better. You can walk without your crutches now. Or hadn't you noticed?'

'You're right, I can!' He stood without support; he managed a few limping but resolute steps and remained on his feet. 'I'm hungry, aren't you?' They had drunk from the stream, but their only food had been a handful of wild strawberries. 'Perhaps I can find some more berries. Or mushrooms. I can tell the poisonous ones. Their bases are swollen cups. I learned that from my father. He uses them in the shop to make ratsbane.'

'You'd better stay here,' she said and then, thinking that possibly she had embarrassed him by her affectionate arm – seventeen-year-old boys did not always like to be hugged by older women – she closed her eyes as if she wished to sleep. He sat beside her and replaced the arm around his shoulder and leaned his head against her cap.

'Stella,' he said, 'your hair feels soft even under that horrible cap. I want Robin to marry you. I didn't at first, even though you had saved our lives. I guess I was jealous. I thought he wouldn't have room for both of us. But he needs you more.'

'He needs us both, Nicholas. Remember when I said that the soul lives in a cottage? My own soul has company. Aster joins me in the houseplace and the kitchen. It's only in the bedroom that I'm alone. But till he found you, Robin had nobody in *any* room except his nieces and nephews and friends, who came and went, but never came to stay. The only one who stayed was that disagreeable sounding pig, Caligula. Now he has company in you.'

'But not in his solar – that's where he keeps his bed. That's where he needs you.'

'I suppose I want too much. I want to be in all his rooms. It's for him to decide, though. If he gives me only the porch, I'll learn to be content.'

'Will you?' he asked doubtfully.

133

Honesty could be a wicked nuisance. Sometimes she wished for Judith's skill at self-deception. 'Maybe not content. At least resigned.'

'For how long?'

'Between my attempts to move into the solar!'

'And what about *my* cottage?' asked Aster. 'Am I to have no company?'

'Be patient, Titmouse. At your age, one shouldn't expect to have every room filled. That's the joy of growing up. Filling room after room.'

'I could use some help.'

'It's awfully late,' said Nicholas. 'Do you think something has happened to Robin?'

'I don't know. Our escape from Dartmoor seemed a little too easy. I won't feel safe until – listen! There's someone coming.'

The young Roman rescued from human sacrifice by her ancestress could not have been half so surprised by joy.

'It's Robin and he's leading two horses!'

'Quickly now,' he cried. 'Stella and Aster, this one's name is Piebald. He's old and he won't gallop but he'll get you to Exeter. Let's hope we won't be pursued.'

Stella was not a stranger to horses. She had ridden to the hounds with Philip, and it seemed to her wonderfully natural to bestride this large, ungainly, but docile beast named Piebald, with Aster riding pillion behind her. Robin and Nicholas had mounted too – a horse by the name of Essex – and Nicholas had thrown away his crutches.

'I won't need you any more!' he shouted to the hateful wood. Artor, roused from his sleep shuffled between the two horses. He growled in the fashion of bears who like their sleep but, swift as a horse, swifter than these old rusticated horses, he would have no trouble keeping pace with them.

'To Exeter!' cried Robin, who ought to be whispering – they still might arouse the town – but how he stirred her blood! To Exeter! To voyages further than Virginia: To lands unguessed by mere, mundane cartographers! Perhaps, at last, to a cottage with more than a porch! According to the ancients, no man steps twice into the same river from the same bank. For her, it was a different river, but it flowed toward the same sea.

But not for long.

Fingers of bracken clawed at her ankles, hands, face. Sharp, brittle, wounding. Had Piebald stumbled into a pit? No, the fingers were crueller than bracken. They belonged to men.

Piebald was not a Pegasus who could spread his wings and lift her and Aster above their enemies, or a Bucephalus who could snort and paw and thunder to Exeter through swords and pikes. Once they had dragged her from the horse, they stood back from her in a circle, like bullies whose numbers gave them superiority but not courage and she saw their faces in the thin light of the moon.

'Bind their hands,' someone was saying. She would have expected Judith. But there were no women in this land of sleepy-eyed farmers from Dean Church, who looked distinctly unmenacing and uncomfortable at having to apprehend their vicar, even if he was in the company of a dubious woman and guiltily fleeing from his own parish.

But they were more than menaced, they were captured; Nicholas' father was leading the captors. Somehow, Judith had sent or brought him word of the escape. He had gathered a band of farmers; waited for Robin in the town; followed him to the hiding place of his friends; and apprehended them once they had mounted their horses.

He was carrying a pike, a curious weapon for an apothecary, but not unbecoming to his lordly stance, his air of being about the Lord's business.

Robin, who knocked down three men before being knocked to his knees and bound with the leather thongs which the farmers used on their sheep, glared up at his captors – his particular captor – and boomed in the voice he used on a sleepy congregation.

'Has the devil possessed you, Standish? I'm taking your son to Exeter to find a physician. His leg has worsened and—'

For answer, the Apothecary drove his pike into Artor's heart.

The dragonfly moon sank below the horizon. Dawn ruddied the sky. Cocks began to crow; a simple, homely sound that moved her to tears because it was with just such homely things – an old mill, a trundle bed, a garden where hollyhocks grew among the beets – that she had filled her life since Philip's death and made a series of little magics between the large sadnesses, the dreads and the angers. All night she had lain on her side, hands and feet bound behind her, wakeful and waiting. She did not know the place; she only knew that she lay atop a hill, with a farmer standing guard above her; she could hear Robin, Nicholas, and Aster breathing on the same hill, but at some distance from her. Not so far, though, that she could not distinguish between their breaths, Robin's deep and long; Nicholas' light and sporadic – if he slept he dreamed bad dreams. Only Aster appeared to be sleeping with the innocence and, thank Picus, the ignorance of a child.

Once, in that interminable time between the death of the moon and the birth of dawn, she called a name:

'Robin!'

'Stella, I'm here.'

'Hush, Mistress. You are not to speak to him.'

'Where are we?' she asked her guard.

'Oh the Hill.'

'Which hill?'

'The Hill of Stakes.'

'Where you burn witches?'

'Yes.'

'One last year. Two in '28. That's all.' He stood behind her and she could not see him, but her ears had already told her that he was young and reluctant.

'Will you light the fires?'

'Oh, no, Mistress Stella.' He had heard Robin speak her name.

'Will you watch?'

'Yes. Hush now. They're bringing the stakes.'

Trussed like a calf for branding, she could not turn her head to watch the climbers. To judge from the sound, there must be twenty or more men and some of them seemed to be carrying heavy objects; they gasped and paused from time to time and resumed their climb. Soon she heard them digging around their bases. At first she wished that her ears had been as dull as her nostrils; no, she was not an ostrich. Better to hear the preparations, shovel and hammer and shovel, than to lie in silence, looking at the earth and imagining horrors more horrible than the truth.

The young guard severed her thongs with a knife which looked as if it were made for whittling toys and lifted her to her feet. His hands jerked and trembled; perhaps he was afraid to touch her. He was a farmer, to judge from his tunic, his low boots, and the leather lacings around his calves.

Her feet felt dead; at first they could not support her weight. 'Please,' she said. 'The blood has left my feet.' He averted his eyes when she looked at him (he thinks I will give him the evil eye). He was not a Puritan, certainly not a Gubbing. His hair was as black and unkempt as a crow from a haystack. His red countenance was open, potentially blithe, not unintelligent. She liked him.

'No,' she said. 'I think I can stand.'

He gave her his hand. 'Are you—?'

'A witch? No more than your sweetheart or mother.'

He shook his head. 'Master Standish says—' But at least she caught his eye.

'You're crying,' he said. 'Witches can't cry.' He dropped her hand and clambered down the hill.

She felt a surprising loss with his going; she who had so much more to lose. At least she had time to study the place of her death. The light of early morning was preter-naturally clear, or perhaps desperation sharpened her senses. In Dean Church, there was neither a town square nor a village green. Witches were burned on a hill which overlooked the town. Below, the quiet stone cottages with their vines and roses were chattering into life. The flutter of sparrows under the eaves (a female has broken her wing); the cry of a child (not hurt – he wants attention); the bark of an old sheep dog, (rheumatism has settled in his legs). She could see much; she could hear everything. Probably Robin could smell the breads and puddings, the hogsback and bacon of breakfast.

Here, the wind-swept hill, devoid of trees, sparse of grass, thrust its stakes into the sky like slender living pines. The hill should be proud. At last it had grown a semblance of a tree. Robin, Nicholas, and Aster, each under guard, stood widely separated and at some distance from her.

The young farmer, of course, had not left her unguarded. There were perhaps a dozen men on the hill, and they ranged in mood from frightened to frightening:

138

a timorous shepherd who looked as if he might mistake a scarecrow's shadow for a devil. Scobble and Scobble's father, identical except that the father was as brown and wrinkled as a maple leaf in fall; identical in their slow, shuffling gait and in their faces, which were capable of two expressions; cupidity and stupidity.

'Why is my child here?' she called to Scobble's father. 'Children aren't burned. Even convicted witches are usually hanged before they are burned.'

He blinked and stared at her. 'Burn them here in Dean Church, we do. Too much waste to build a gallows first.' He fingered the wart on the lobe of his left ear. 'For the girl, it's drowning, though.' He pointed to a stream which ran prettily beside the hill, between willows, among reeds; deep in places; translucent like the fins of an angel fish. 'She can see the burning first.'

'She isn't a witch. She—' A sudden slap caught her across the mouth. It was not Scobble's father, who lacked the courage to strike a witch. It was Michael Standish.

He spoke loudly enough for everyone on the hill to hear him. 'It is universally acknowledged that the daughter of a witch becomes a witch.' Then, in a whisper audible only to the ears of a Gubbing, 'The daughter of a traitress becomes a traitress.' She understood his loathing for her and Aster. She had fled to Exeter and, in spite of her return, continued to walk in that subtle aura of freedom which was like a wind from the Channel, salt-fresh, invigorating, intoxicating. He had journeyed to London and found a city to hate and condemn, a modern Sodom which the Lord had spared for reasons to be found not even in the Book of Redemption. Its bishops and courtiers? A band of Satyrs from whom an eternity in Hell was insufficient punishment. Its King? A weakling and, worse, a Papist in disguise.

Stella had always known that he was a Gubbing; she

139

had known him when she was a little girl and he and his wife had left for London 'on God's work'. She had known Nicholas, too, as a baby in Dartmoor, orphaned by the Plague and placed with the Standishes when they returned from London to Dean Church (and surreptitiously, when they could, to Dartmoor) and introduced as their son. The Gubbings lost no chance to place orphans with their own people who were infiltrating the towns and cities of England and the colonies of the New World. In a few instances, the placing had been detected and the child, stripped, examined, exposed with wings or feathers, was taken to be a changeling and drowned in the nearest stream. In Nicholas' case, the Standishes had arrived in Dean Church with him and no one had guessed that they were not his true parents. Since he was one of those rare Gubbings who possessed no rudiments of wings or feathers, he had not been told the truth; children talk; he might have told his schoolmates. As a youth he was sent to be trained in the ministry at Emmanuel College, the Puritan stronghold at Cambridge. At a suitable time – if he had betrayed Robin, for example, and after completing his studies – he would have been told about his origins, taken to Dartmoor for instruction – and instructions – and sent into the unenlightened world as yet another Puritan to teach that God was duty, not love, and duty lay in burning witches, (unless they were faithful Gubbings) and conspiring against King Charles, his wordly courtiers, and his ritualistic bishops.

Stella had hesitated to tell Nicholas that he was a Gubbing. The boy lacked confidence. A few days with Robin had already lessened his sense of sin, but to learn that he was one of those same beings who had almost crucified him and his friend might have crippled him more than the hooves of that ramping horse in Cambridge.

She had meant to tell Robin. He would have forgiven

the boy; no, forgiveness implied judgment, and Robin accepted and did not judge Nicholas. But she and Robin, when they had not been with Aster and Nicholas, had talked about marriage, and the subject had proved not only explosive but exclusive: like talk of the winds and the sea on a tempest-threatened ship, or talk of fire in a burning town.

Now Nicholas' foster father was coolly preparing to execute him. The boy had failed him as a spy, as a Puritan, as a Gubbing; he was weak, he was sinful, and he had been to Dartmoor for the wrong reasons. He must be destroyed, if not as a warlock, then as a witch's minion. Stella would carry him with her to her own death, along with Robin and Aster.

Except for Mistress Standish and the young farmer who had guarded her through the night, the entire populace of Dean Church, it seemed, had come to watch the burnings. There must have been three hundred people who climbed the hill – parents carrying babies, children scrambling ahead of their parents. It might have been a holiday, it might have been a hanging. It was hard to tell from that wall of grinning, ghoulish faces.

Humans, she thought, with infinite revulsion; with the ancient lordly prejudice of her people when they had flown in the clouds and built their homes in the trees and literally looked down on human men and women. She was a Skyking; she was a sky queen. And yet these humans had dared to humble and humiliate her, Stella, whose ancestors had been worshipped as gods, celebrated as kings; whose ancestress had graced the Book of Rejoicing.

Humans.

But Robin was a human. Furthermore, what her people had become was surely lower than what these people had been born. As they reached the top of the hill she saw that they were not, after all, indistinguishable. Indeed, there were ghouls, who feasted with their eyes if not their lips. That youth with the hump on his back: had his deformity withered his compassion? His mouth was agape with a drooling grin. And the curiosity-seekers, heartless if not quite murderous. That woman with the straw-colored bonnet. Chirping to her neighbor as if she had entered some tarts in a county fair and come to watch the tasting. But by and large she saw in the faces not so much cruelty, nor even curiosity, as far; not so much the will to wound as the wish to be guarded against diabolical spells. They were afraid of her. A witch. A Satanist. They did not really want to torture or punish her. They wanted to free themselves from her threat in a fashion which, they supposed, would also dispose of her ghost and free them from future hauntings. The soul of a witch who was hanged might haunt the countryside for a hundred years. The soul of a witch who was burned was thought to sink immediately into Hell.

She understood them but she did not forgive them. She was not a simpering Christian to turn the other cheek (but then, what Christian truly practiced his creed?). She was a Skyking. 'Lose your talons, strike with your beak!' Thus, the Book of Rejoicing. They were going to drown her daughter. They were going to burn her friends. Their deeds if not their souls were cruel. Most of the world's harm, it seemed, was done by ignorant, essentially decent men. The Spanish Inquisitors had burned a heretic and gone to church or played on the green with their children.

Picus, let them get on with their unintentional evil, their deadly decency! Or give me the evil eye that they fear and let me strike them blind! At least you can say for the Gubbings that they farm badly, mine with indifference, but crucify with a skill approaching art.

She was strangely pleased to see that Nicholas' foster-mother had not come to the burning. Probably she was the only inhabitant of Dean Church to remain in her home. Judith had come, of course. Judith was bound to come. She had lifted her cape as if to protect her face on that brisk and windy morning. She looked like an upright shadow, and no more threatening. A traveler from a neighboring town? Somebody's aunt or cousin from London? What did it matter? Burnings, even if sudden, always attracted strangers. No one would question her.

Judith looked into her eyes and smiled: You went to Exeter and see where it led. . . .

Stella did not envy her; she did not even hate her: I took the road to Exeter. Twice. Shall I protest that this time I did not reach the sea? It is journeys and not destinations which have made me rich. My innocent child must die in pain, but she has lived for nine years in my love. To save her life, I would wish her not my child. But I would not wish her yours.

There had not as yet been a trial. Even in this, the cruelest era of witch-burning England had ever known, witches were never burned without a trial. Little Dean Church could boast neither judge nor mayor, and no one had taken time to invite magistrates from Exeter. But Michael Standish, it seemed, intended to follow the King's law. He himself would enact the role of judge, and the townspeople would be his jurors.

The stakes had been raised, the faggots heaped to resemble hayricks; but there were doubts in the minds of the people. Downcast eyes, a furtive blink, doubt and perplexity. They were not a compassionate folk, they were not an intelligent folk; but by and large they did not wish to burn their vicar and a boy from their own village unless there was irrefutable proof of their guilt. Stella and Aster were strangers to them; curiosities. But Robin had preached in their own church. They had fallen asleep in his sermons. Some of them had accused him of demonic practices. But girls had loved him, boys had imitated him, mothers had baked him pies. Coming from London, a poet, a man of learning before he was a man of God, he had been resented. He had also been respected; by some, adored. Michael Standish, august and judicial, was not at this moment a popular man.

He must have anticipated resistance. He must have known that the only powers he possessed were those which were lent to him by superstition and hysteria. He had presumed to lead the townfolk of Dean Church and till now they had followed him, even to the Hill of Burnings. But presumption could lead to a fall. Now he was a judge; if he managed to condemn Stella and her friends, he would become a kind of hero; disliked but still heroic. If he failed to condemn her he would be, what he had been, a rich apothecary, but also less than he had been, reviled instead of respected.

She watched him watching the crowd and assessing their mood; judging the precise moment to make his accusation. She shivered but not with the cold. The prettily winding river caught the glint of the sun and held her eye ... images crowded and chilled her brain ... Philip's beloved Shakespeare ... doubting Hamlet ... doomed Ophelia ...

(There is a willow grows askant the brook
That shows his hoar leaves in the glassy stream,
Therewith fantastic garlands did she make. ...)

He raised his hands. Armored in righteous arrogance, he managed to silence even that motley and divided group.

'You will wonder,' he said, 'why I have summoned you here. I am not a judge. I am not a messenger of the king or an official servant of the Church. I have no authority but that which is granted to all God-fearing men by the Deity, who may work for good through the humblest of his subjects.' (Humility did not become him; his listeners had not come to hear a sermon. He hastened to more dramatic pronouncements.) 'I have called you here to judge a woman I believe to be a witch. A child who must share her mother's guilt. Our Vicar, Robert Herrick, who was apprehended with them on the road to Exeter.' He faltered and momentarily seemed to lose his voice; he brushed an invisible tear from his cheek. 'And my own misguided son.' There was no visible response from the crowd. He held their attention but he had not won their sympathy. He was still a parishioner condemning his vicar and a father condemning his son. 'Perhaps I am mistaken; I hope that I am mistaken. But if I am right, I need hardly tell you the consequences if the woman is freed. There is witchcraft practiced in Dartmoor, of that we can have no doubt. Mysterious lights. Disappearances. Deaths. Shall we return a witch to her coven? Allow me to quote from a sermon preached to Queen Elizabeth by one of her most respected bishops.' (Elizabeth, dead for twenty-seven years, was a demon to Gubbings but a saint to Anglicans.)

May it please your Grace to understand that witches and Sorcerers within these few years are marvelously increased within your Grace's realm. Your Grace's subjects pine away even unto the death; their colour fadeth, their flesh rotteth, their speech is benumbed, their senses are bereft. . . .

Rotting flesh, fading cheeks — cruelty familiar to anyone who had lost a child or spouse to the Plague.

'Is this woman guilty of such atrocities?' It was the Miller's wife. Doubtless Standish had asked her to ask the question. As carefully as the ministers of Queen Elizabeth had arranged a masque or a progress, he had calculated a performance extending from the capture on the road to Exeter through the burning of his captives, and he must not seem to be the sole performer.

He crossed the hill; he paused in front of Stella and turned on her a look which both accused and besought; that of a saint exhorting a sinner to repent. Then he addressed her in a measured, mesmerizing voice, the voice which men use to tame wild animals, or to win crowds who are more sincere than intelligent.

'You have heard my charge. What have you to say in your own defense, Mistress Stella?'

She wanted to spit in his eye, but it would hardly help her defense.

'If a witch is a woman who serves the devil, I am innocent. If she performs spells, rots flesh, benumbs speech – I am innocent. And even if I were guilty, my daughter and my friends—'

With the swiftness of a viper -- and how the old Skykings had hated the vipers which had threatened their eggs! – his hand leaped to her head, bared her of cap and hood, and liberated her hair, that tumult richer than roses, too crimson to be angelic. She knew for the first time what men had told her – Philip, Robin, and others – that she was more than comely, that she was beautiful in the high, legendary sense of Helen, who had destroyed a city, and Deirdre, whom love had destroyed. Here on this little hill, this mockery of a Troy, she was still her own legend. The men desired her and the women envied her. Thus had Standish worked her destruction. Great beauty was either worshipped or defiled. Men would murder what they desired and could not possess. Women would murder what they envied and could not attain.

'She must be a witch,' cried Corinna. 'Why, look at that hair! The Devil gave it those fires.'

It was Robin who answered her; it was Robin whom Standish allowed to answer her. The subtlety with which he controlled the trial was evident to Stella, his countrywoman, but to the crowd it must have seemed that he was acting the part of the fair-minded judge; hearing all possible argument; reserving judgment.

Robin's voice was hot with controlled anger. The lavas were held in check, but the least crack and a mountain would burst into fire.

'King James had decreed and King Charles had confirmed witches shall die for necromancy, laming, wasting men's bodies or goods, and harboring familiar spirits. Furthermore, judges shall not condemn on hearsay. At Leicester, nine people were condemned on the word of a small boy who was subject to fits. James himself intervened and freed the accused. What is your proof against Mistress Stella?'

'That bear of hers – a familiar, I'll warrant.'

'He's dead. Standish killed him with one thrust of his pike. A familiar you say?'

' 'Tisn't hearsay my cow sickened the night of the Harvest Home and died next day. Healthiest animal in the barn!'

'Three of my hens died the same night.'

'A horse ran down my dog.'

It was Standish himself who answered the indignant farmers. 'Our Vicar is right. There are intimations of guilt, but as yet no proof. Least of all the woman's beauty. Beauty alone does not betoken a witch. Consider Ruth and Esther, Rebecca and even Rahab, the harlot. Yet each in her own way followed God's path.'

Having exposed her as beautiful and therefore suspect, he had surprisingly defended her. He had silenced the crowd in its outcries. Thus, when he made his final and fatal charge, he would seem to have been an impartial judge who had deliberated in his own conscience, resisting the haste of the crowd; seeing excuses for the woman until the disclosure of that which was inexcusable.

'But there is, after all, further evidence. Irrefutable evidence.' He lifted her hair and rested his hand on the back of her neck. A viper, she thought. Cold, in spite of his body heat; stained and seamed from the powders he mixes, the roots he digs in his herbarium. If he does not take it away—

He removed his hand. He also removed the back of her gown and petticoat in one rending jerk. Thus, swiftly, simply, and irrevocably, he exposed her to the waist. He exposed her as a witch.

'Crimson like her hair. Is it part of her petticoat?'

'Petticoat! It's wings. The woman has wings!'

'Like a griffin.'

'No. Like a phoenix!'

Before they have finished with me, I will welcome the flames, she thought. The English are kinder to witches than the Swiss or the French. As a rule they hang them before they burn them, but out of kindness, not cruelty, and they do not flay them or lop off their ears and fingers. But these Englishmen have seen my wings, which are ugly and stunted like my people. And Robin has seen them, Robin who thought them tall like flames, the wings of a queen. I know how Lucifer felt when he fell from heaven.

The sound of their voices came to her as if from the uppermost branches of a tall oak tree: muffled, distant, distorted. Perhaps she dreamed them. Surely she dreamed them.

'But her wings are unfolding like flames! How did she hide them under her gown?'

'They're slender, you see. Tapering and delicate. The bodice pressed them against her back.'

'Can she fly, do you think?'

'She doesn't need to fly. It's enough to look like Lilith. If she flew, she would be an angel.'

'Is she evil then?'

'Yes. But men could die for her.'

'That is her evil.'

She remembered lines from the Book of Rejoicing: 'And her love was so great that her wings stood tall like flames. . . .'

'Tall like flames' . . . It was true then. It was also true that she stood condemned.

In the almost-hush of her beauty, she spoke to the crowd:

'You have seen my wings. If they make me a witch, then he' – she pointed at Michael Standish – 'and he' – at the Miller – 'and he' – at the Blacksmith – 'and she' – at the Seamstress – 'must share in my guilt. They are my own people. Winged like me. Strip them and see for yourselves.'

For one tenuous moment, for one drip of a water clock, it seemed that the crowd would listen to her. The Miller, the Seamstress, the Blacksmith – they looked as if she had lashed them in the face with a myrtle rod. Indeed, she had lashed them with fear. They could not have known that Michael Standish, at incalculable risk, would reveal her wings and give her the chance to make her own accusations.

But Standish answered her with the unanswerable argument: laughter. He, the dour Puritan apothecary, threw back his head and laughed like a jovial cavalier. 'A warlock. She calls me a warlock. Shall I strip for you here on this hill? Do you want to see the naked limbs of your apothecary? White, skinny, hairless. Wings, did she say? Anna, who sews your aprons – a *witch*! Good Master Thomas, your blacksmith, a *warlock*! Perhaps he charms your horses into losing their shoes to increase his business.'

'She'll have us all witches!' It was the Seamstress.

'Or warlocks,' It was Scobble.

Michael Standish had hurled his deadliest pike. It had struck in her heart because the people of Dean Church did not want to believe that their town had been infiltrated by a band of winged Satanists. It was one thing to burn a witch and her two minions and drown her daughter and then return to their fields and their looms. But the Miller, the Seamstress, the Blacksmith, even the Apothecary. Must the hill be forested with stakes? And so they howled in a frenzy of merriment, and she shut her eyes and wished for once that she could close her ears.

In the cloudless sky, a great white falcon wheeled in diminishing arcs.

They hurried her toward the stake. Pulled, prodded, dragged by the hand (but no one touched her wings). She might have been a great queen taken in adultery.

She stood almost as tall as the stake (frugal, these farmers. Why should they waste their wood?). She felt the faggots thrust against her ankles, her legs, her breast. They should have been placed in a carefully measured circle around her, waist-high, without quite touching her. The victim was meant to suffocate from the smoke before she was burned to death. But they piled the branches as high as her neck and pressed them cruelly into her skin. They wanted to hide her wings. They were still afraid of her.

Clumsy murderers, they cannot even burn me without their perpetual bumbling clumsiness. Picus, let them be gentle with Aster when they drown her!

(..... *Her clothes spread wide,*
And mermaid-like, awhile they bore her up;
Which time she chanted snatches of old lauds,
As one incapable of her own distress.)

It would be a kindness to suffocate her while she slept. I have heard of such kindnesses even among humans. If someone could only hear me! If I could speak above this babble of threats, exorcisms, jeers!

Strange, this God of the Christians, at least what his worshippers do in his name. In place of joy, this—

'I want to light his fire.' Scobble advanced upon Robin with swaggering steps while his father watched with paternal pride. 'He beat me up in the fields. Some of you saw him. Now we know what he is.'

'Look,' cried Corinna, pointing to the sky. 'Is it an eagle?'

'Big enough to be. But no. The hooked, notched bill — And he doesn't soar; his wings beat all the time.'

'And the white feathers – a gyrfalcon.'

'Too far south.'

'Storms blow them down.'

'But the size of the fellow. Never seen one so large!'

'Now you have!'

The bird descended in rapid, lessening arcs. Sunlight glittered yellowly in his eyes. She could hear his wing-beats, rhythmic and unhurried. As if he had sighted his prey and judged him to be entrapped. A rabbit in a field without a warren. A serpent asleep in the sun. Scobble stared at him until the resin began to run down his arm.

Michael Standish took the torch from his hand. 'The woman should be the first to burn, my son.' Mosaic, omnipotent, he gestured toward the bird as if he were bidding the waters of the Red Sea to part. 'God sent doves to signal the end of the flood. Now he has sent a falcon to witness the burning of a woman with wings. What creature could be more fitting?'

The bird seemed almost bodiless when he dove; almost invisible; a mist of sunlight and cloud and feathers. The awesomeness, the awfulness had momentarily gone from him. But when he struck he was a hardness of rock and bronze, talons to rend, a beak to tear, and a wingspread as wide as Nicholas with outstretched arms!

Standish dropped the torch and threw up his hands to protect his face. He forgot to protect his back.

His cape, his shirt, his undergarment of brown sack-cloth – had they too dissolved in the sun? Torn from his back in a single beat of those wings, they slid to the ground behind him like a dying fox. There were no wings to billow from his own shoulders, no wonder of leaping flame, but his back was aflame with russet feathers, a miracle of glittering plumage. It seemed at first yet another garment, a finely woven fabric of softest silk. But the merciless, merciful sun distinguished the individual feathers of a Gubbing.

He did not try to hide his nakedness. He faced the crowd with the arrogant dignity of an angel prepared to fall for the second time.

(*A tall shadow flickered down the hill.*)

Book Five: Aster

CHAPTER XII

ASTER loved weddings. She had always known that, having missed the first, she would love her mother's second wedding. But who would have thought that anyone *thirty* could have looked like a handmaiden to the Lark Goddess? Mama's hair was drawn into a loose knot behind her head, but crimson ringlets fell like rose petals over her bare shoulders. Her cloak of white velvet, held by an emerald clasp, rippled like wind-stirred foliage above her gown of pale green satin and above her slippers which peeped from the hem like snails and led Robin to compose a verse with the speed of Mother Goose (or perhaps to quote a verse which he had already composed):

> *Her pretty feet*
> *Like snails did creep*
> *A little out, and then,*
> *As if they started at Bo-Peep,*
> *Did soon draw in again.*

At her throat, a malachite pendant hung in the shape of a soaring Pegasus, and at her back her wings extended like tapering flames whose tips brushed the rushes on the floor.

Robin, though he had not lost his ability to compose, lost his composure at the start of the ceremony. Aster was not surprised. The poor man had suffered unspeakable dangers, unmentionable indignities, the past week. That terrible morning on the hill, when those dirty, rough-handed farmers had meant to burn him and dear Mama and Nicholas, and drown *her*, but ended by burning the Apothecary, the Seamstress, the Blacksmith, the Miller and his beet-faced wife, Scobble and father, and at least a dozen other disguised Gubbings (and later, she was told, they had drowned three children in the same stream where she herself was supposed to end). When the falcon had plummeted out of the sky like a warrior of Picus and ripped the Apothecary's shirt and bared his plumage, you would have thought that the Spaniards had landed a second Armada. Shouts. Accusations. Protestations. Scufflings on the ground. Some of the people had started to run from the hill, but others had overtaken and undressed them right down to their stockings. Some had wings, some had plumage like the Apothecary; some, bare-backed and black of hair, and therefore presumed innocent, were allowed to reclaim their clothes, or what was left of them, and undress their neighbors. In order to avoid the indignity of ripped clothes and searching hands, many had undressed themselves – that shameless Corinna had pranced over the hill with breasts aquiver like Christmas puddings tipped with cherries – and you would have thought that they were planning an orgy around a Maypole. In less than an hour the hill was forested with stakes and there was a forest fire which Aster had mercifully been spared; a farmwife had taken her into the village; but Michael Standish was said to have made the biggest blaze and never once had he lost his Moses look.

Hardly had the flames fallen to ashes than the able bodied men and boys of Dean Church seized their shepherd staffs and hammers and matchlocks and marched on Dartmoor, through the bracken, around the pits, into the village, into the Tabernacle. But there was no one anywhere in the town. There was food on some of the tables, there were fires on some of the hearths. But Judith had fled with all of her people to spread their mischief throughout the land. Perhaps they would find a ship and sail to Plymouth or found a new colony and shame the Indians out of their loin cloths and into trousers. At least they would no longer wander Dartmoor at night with lanters like Will-o-the-Wisps, and eat horses, and crucify men and women near Dean Church.

That Mama and Nicholas had not been burned and that she herself had not been drowned was a sheer miracle, said Nicholas. No, said Robin. It was belated justice. The townfolk had understood that they were trying to escape from their own people, that they were renouncing them and their harsh, loveless, perverted ways. She and Mama were adjudged repentant and therefore redeemed witches, and Nicholas, a repentant and redeemed warlock, and Robin was commended for having helped them in their escape.

There had followed a long consultation between Robin and the town elders – those who had not been burned – and the elders had decided first of all that it was unwise to alarm the bishop at Exeter with tales which he might not believe, and wise to spread the word that the Plague had made a sudden visit to Dean Church. Second, that Robin could keep his parish. However, it was unthinkable for him to marry Mama. She could hide her 'Sinfully beautiful' hair under a bonnet, wear unpretentious clothes, become his servant, and live with Aster and Nicholas in his gatehouse. Every vicar needed a servant. Robin's vicarage could do with some cleaning, what with that disreputable pig about the place, and he could also use a cook. Mama was forgiven and accepted, Robin was rewarded by an increase in salary from twenty-eight to thirty pounds a year, but a vicar and a Gubbing, even a redeemed Gubbing, simply could not marry and remain in Dean Church. Furthermore, Mama would have to change her name. Corinna's father suggested 'Prudence Baldwin' after an aunt who had died a presumed virgin at the age of ninety-three. 'It smacks of virtue. It ought to keep her redeemed.'

'If I can't marry her here, we'll go away and be married,' Robin had told the elders (or so he had told Mama).

'But where else will you be safe?' they had argued. 'There are no more Gubbings around Dean Church. But from what you say, there may be Gubbings everywhere else in the country, and even in Virginia and Massachusetts. It's keep your parish and safety, or go wandering and probably be crucified along with your woman and her little girl and poor fatherless Nicholas.' (Nicholas's foster mother had escaped from Dean Church before the burnings and become, so Aster had later heard, a harlot in Exeter like Mama's old friend. Harlotry sounded like a stimulating, if insecure, profession. She understood that it was rather like being the Whore of Babylon.)

Robin had repeated his talk with the elders to Mama, who had said at once, 'But of course you must stay in Dean Church. The people are just starting to appreciate you. They'll listen to your sermons now, even if you quote Catullus.'

'You really think so, Stella?'

'Of course I do, my dear. "Prudence Baldwin" will suit me very well for a name. And you know how I love to cook. You're sure your parishioners won't talk, though, about my living in the gate-house?'

'Oh, some of the women will gossip a bit. But everybody knows the circumstances. And now that the Gubbings are gone, these country folk are a pretty realistic bunch. When you grow up with cows and pigs and chickens, you know that people, even vicars, sometimes have to make – er – arrangements. For the sake of appearances, you can keep your things in the gate-house, but of course you'll sleep in my trundle bed. And not in the trundle. Furthermore, we can slip off from time to time to the mill. Even a vicar has his holidays.'

'What about Caligula?'

'He can sleep in the gate-house.'

'And we can have our own private arrangements, can't we, Robin, our own private ceremony in the mill and *really* be married in the eyes of Picus and the Lark Goddess and Mother Goose.'

The mill was rainbowed with flowers – those little mothlike daisies that grew among the bracken, hollyhocks from Stella's garden and roses from the Vicarage, and especially sunflowers, heaped on the table with the mince pies and the mulled cider and scattered over the floor along with the rushes. It was a private ceremony. Weddings among the old Skykings had always been private, with no one invited except the family and closest friends. Robin had wanted to invite his nieces and nephews. Aster heard him muttering something to Nicholas about 'safety in numbers', whatever that meant. But he had decided that there were far too many of them to get in the mill.

'Nicholas,' he had said, 'if I invite one, I'll have to invite all of them, and their mothers and fathers too. So I'm not going to invite anybody but you. But you can ask your best friend, if you like.'

'But that's you,' said Nicholas.

'Second best?'

'George.'

George rode from Cambridge on a snorting black stallion whose hoofbeats sounded like thunder and whose mane was as black as a thunder-cloud. It was Aster who held the reins and helped him to dismount (not that he needed help; it seemed a courtesy, though, to give him her hand.) Of course he was even older than Nicholas, but Pegasus, what a man! A cavalier, that's what he was. She had never seen such golden hair except on Robin, but George's hair was fashionably combed and curled and, she supposed, lamenting her undeveloped nostrils, perfumed with exotic pomades from the Indies. He wore earrings of hammered gold – what would Judith have thought? – and a lace-edged collar and a scarlet coat with lavendar braids, and boots of jacked leather, and *two* pairs of stockings. And he seemed to fancy her! He called her 'my little Titmouse' and he patted her on the head and promised to bring her a pomander bracelet from London, and it seemed to her that he was saying in his gentlemanly way, 'None of the London girls can hold a feather to you! I don't mind the wait.'

She did not want to disappoint Nicholas; truly he was a good and loyal friend. But you had to choose a husband who could, as her mother had said, fill all the rooms of your cottage. Nicholas would understand. At the proper time, she would help him to find his own bride. One of those rustic girls, perhaps nimble at the loom and quick in the kitchen.

The ceremony was brief and simple. Mama and Robin joined hands and read together from the Book of Rejoicing.

Let acorns cornucopia-heap our table, let the clouds through which we frolic never resound with thunder or crackle with lightnings. Let us live as blissfully as turtle doves in an apple tree. In the name of Picus and the Lady of the Larks, of Mother Goose, Pegasus, and all the lesser saints, we are joined together in blissful matrimony, to disport ourselves in amorous dalliance among the treetops and to grace our nest with cinnamon-speckled eggs. . .

After the ceremony, Mama began to cry. Robin did his best to comfort her, though he ended with Nicholas having to comfort *him*. Men were always embarrassed by a woman's tears.

'I'm crying for joy,' Mama insisted. 'The wedding, the excitement. Let me catch my breath on the porch. Then I'll be ready for a hogshead of ale.' Aster was worried, though. It was rare for Mama to cry, whatever the reason. She peeped onto the porch through a crack in the door.

Extraordinary! There was that same white falcon, perched on the railing as if he owned the mill and big enough to defend his claim. Mama had a way with birds and animals. In fact, she was talking to him.

'Is it all right, Philip? Truly?' She must have named him for Aster's father.

Philip flapped his wings and rose thunderously into the sky, circled twice and dipped his head like a sailor greeting a fine London lady, and disappeared into clouds less white than his own foamy feathers.

'Mama,' Aster screamed. 'No, no!' For Mama was climbing onto the rail and, horror of horrors, spreading her wings and *stepping into space*.

It was twelve feet to the ground.

Aster ran to the rail, Nicholas and George behind her, and stared at the ground, expecting to see her mother nursing a broken leg or a sprained ankle.

But Mama was smiling among her hollyhocks at least an apple's throw from the mill.

'Mama, you flew!'

'No, Titmouse. Glided, that's all. Just give me time.'

But where was the bridegroom? Not on the porch with her and Nicholas and George – not in the houseplace – she would have heard him. There, there, running out of the mill and stumbling through the hollyhocks and into Mama's arms!

Aster began to cry.

'What's the matter, Titmouse?' George asked. 'Your mother looks fine to me.'

Men, bless them, never understood these things. She always cried at weddings.

AUTHOR'S NOTE

I wish to express a deep indebtedness to Marjorie Quennell's A History of Everyday Things in England *— both its vivid text and its expert drawings. For the flavor of the early Seventeenth Century I am much indebted to that inimitable novelist, Norah Lofts, and her* Bless This House. *And for the facts of Robert Herrick's life and the folklore of Devon or Devonshire, the county in which he preached, I borrowed often and gratefully from Marchette Chute's* Two Gentle Men.

All of the poems attributed to Herrick are indeed by him, even the uncharacteristic piece quoted, piece meal, in my chapter on the Trial by Rhyme. As for the other characters in the story, Aster, Nicholas, and Stella are invented, but there was a 'Prudence Baldwin' who served as Herrick's maid and is generally thought to have warmed his bed as well as his kitchen. When Cromwell came to power, Herrick lost his parish and went into exile; when Charles II came to the throne, Herrick returned in trumph to his little church in Devonshire and Prudence returned as his maid. One likes to think that she had shared his exile. She appears in several of his poems, among them an epitaph written many years before she died. Actually, she outlived him by four years, but he liked to write epitaphs.

—THOMAS BURNETT SWANN

THE END